The Summer
I Shrank
My Grandmother

YEARLING BOOKS/YOUNG YEARLINGS/YEARLING CLASSICS are designed especially to entertain and enlighten young people. Patricia Reilly Giff, consultant to this series, received her bachelor's degree from Marymount College and a master's degree in history from St. John's University. She holds a Professional Diploma in Reading and a Doctorate of Humane Letters from Hofstra University. She was a teacher and reading consultant for many years, and is the author of numerous books for young readers.

For a complete listing of all Yearling titles, write to
Dell Reader Services,
P.O. Box 1045,
South Holland, IL 60473.

The Summer
I Shrank
My Grandmother

by Elvira Woodruff

drawings by Katherine Coville

A Yearling Book

Published by
Dell Publishing
a division of
Bantam Doubleday Dell Publishing Group, Inc.
1540 Broadway
New York, New York 10036

The trademark Yearling® is registered in the U.S. Patent and Trademark Office.

The trademark Dell® is registered in the U.S. Patent and Trademark Office.

ISBN: 0-440-40640-4

Reprinted by arrangement with Holiday House, Inc.

Printed in the United States of America

June 1992

10   9   8   7   6

CWO

For Jerry, an alchemist extraordinaire,
and he plays the accordion like an angel . . .

E.W.

Chapter 1

"This is the biggest mistake that I've ever made in my whole life!" Nelly Brown moaned.

"It's a pretty big one," her cousin Ben agreed. "I've never seen anyone disappear before," he whispered. "I wonder where they go."

Nelly was too stunned to reply. The baby they were watching was almost transparent now. Nelly's lower lip began to tremble. Seeing someone disappear in front of you was bad enough, she decided, but when that someone was your grandmother, and your grandmother was an infant, it was just too horrible!

"She's going, Nell!" Ben said, fighting back tears. "She's almost gone!"

"Don't go, Grandma!" Nelly cried. "This is all my fault . . . all my fault." It was true. If it hadn't been for Nelly and the scientific formula she'd made, her grandmother would still be looking like her solid, seventy-year-old self. But soon, thanks to Nelly's experiment, Emma Brown would be looking like nothing at all!

"I'm sorry, Grandma, I'm so sorry," Nelly whispered.

She wiped away a tear that had rolled down her cheek, trying to remember how it had all started, before her grandmother had gotten this way, before they'd come to the cottage in Seaview. It all began back in April, when her grandmother was still very much a solid person. Nelly remembered how Emma Brown had stopped smiling when she'd heard of her son and daughter-in-law's plans to take Nelly with them to New York State for the summer.

"All the way across the country for two months?" her grandmother had cried out. "Why, you can't deprive me of my only granddaughter for two long months! Besides, who will look after Nelly while you two are up to your ears in seaweed?"

Nelly's parents were marine biologists, and their trip was not to be a vacation as much as a trip to do research.

"It's true, we *will* be awfully busy on this

trip. There won't be much time for sight-seeing." Nelly's father looked at his wife.

"And Nelly *will* have to spend a lot of time with a baby-sitter." Nelly's mother frowned.

"That's it, it's settled. Nelly will spend the summer with me. I've rented a little cottage in Seaview. It will be just perfect for the two of us," Emma Brown declared.

"Yippee!" Nelly hooted from the other side of the living room, where she had been quietly dipping the *TV Guide* into the aquarium. She was conducting an experiment to see whether the fish would read it or eat it.

"Can we take Rugbee with us?" Nelly asked. Rugbee was her grandmother's old dog. He was part collie and part Lab and "mostly lazy," as Emma Brown often said. "And can Ben come, too?"

"Of course we'll take Rugbee," her grandmother answered. "But Ben can't come. He has to visit his dad in Arizona, remember?"

Ben was Nelly's first cousin. They had grown up next door to each other until his parents had divorced. Then, because his mother had decided to go back to school, they had moved close to a college, an hour away. Ben's dad was now living in Arizona and Ben was planning on spending the summer with

him. Nelly missed her cousin and still thought of him as her best friend.

"We'll have a good time, you'll see," Nelly's grandmother said, noticing Nelly's disappointment. "It will be ladies only, though we'll have to make an exception for Mr. Rugbee." She laughed.

"Are you sure you want Nelly for the whole summer?" asked Nelly's father, beckoning his daughter and the soggy *TV Guide* away from the aquarium. "You know she can be quite a handful."

"I know nothing of the kind," Emma Brown said, making room for Nelly on the couch. "She's just a happy, healthy ten-year-old with an inquisitive mind. Actually, she reminds me of the way I used to be. I was ten years old once, too, you know." She smiled at Nelly and playfully gave her curly brown hair a tug.

"You may have been ten once, Mother, but I'm sure your parents never had to put up with the kind of messes this ten-year-old makes," Nelly's mother said, moaning. "Why, just last night she was trying to invent a new kind of spaghetti that would glow in the dark."

"I almost had it glowing," Nelly protested, "but you made me stop."

"The only thing that was glowing was the

huge mess in my kitchen," her mother said wearily.

"I'm surprised at you two." Emma Brown turned to face Nelly's parents. "You should be doing all you can to encourage this child's curiosity," she scolded.

"Believe me, Mother, she needs no encouragement in that department." Nelly's father laughed.

And so, after a bit more discussion, it was decided that Nelly would spend the summer with her grandmother. Nelly gave out a whoop, since Emma Brown was the kind of grandmother that kids dream about. However, most kids don't dream about turning their grandmothers into disappearing infants! Even Nelly Brown hadn't thought of that, although her head was full of other kinds of experiments as she began packing for the trip.

Chapter 2

Nelly had been counting the days till it was time to leave for Seaview. When that Saturday morning finally arrived, she was up and waiting by the front door, before her parents had even come down for breakfast.

"Good grief, Nelly," her father sighed, coming down the stairs. "Grandma has a station wagon, not a moving van!" He surveyed all the boxes stacked up around the door. "You can't take your whole lab with you."

"But, Dad, you're the one who's always talking about finding inspiration wherever you go. What if I get to Seaview and I'm suddenly inspired to come up with a new formula? I'll need some beakers and test tubes," Nelly explained.

"That's fine," her mother said, following

Nelly's father down the stairs. "But when you find yourself inspired to take a swim, you aren't going to be able to put on a beaker or a test tube. You do have to make room for a bathing suit and some clothes, you know."

They spent the rest of the morning unpacking a few of Nelly's boxes and filling three suitcases full of clothes. When her mother reached for another box to unpack, Nelly put her foot down. "Either I get to take the rest of my lab equipment or I don't go," she said firmly.

When Emma Brown arrived, she just smiled knowingly in the direction of Nelly's boxes and opened the back of the station wagon. Nelly picked up a box and carried it to the car with a grin.

"This is going to be a great vacation, Grandma," Nelly said, waving good-bye to her parents from the front seat of the station wagon. Her grandmother stopped at a supermarket to buy some groceries and then they drove the two hours to Seaview, talking about Nelly's experiments along the way. They were still discussing them that night at the cottage.

"I want to invent something brand-new, something no one else has thought of," Nelly said to her grandmother, as she carefully unpacked her beakers and bottles on the kitchen floor. Rugbee grumpily made his way through the maze of glassware and found his doggy bowl in the corner.

Nelly had gotten her first chemistry set when she was seven. It had been love at first sight. To be a scientist, to mix potions, to swirl chemicals, to invent something new and wonderful, Nelly couldn't imagine wanting to do anything else.

When her parents had realized that she was serious, they'd bought her several more advanced chemistry sets, until she had tried them all. Finally her father had begun buying her glassware, beakers, and test tubes from a chemical supply company. The chemistry set she and her father had put together was now made up of professional laboratory equipment. Nelly Brown was on her way to becoming a serious scientist!

"How about edible Play-Doh?" Nelly asked her grandmother excitedly. "Or a hair stunting shampoo? You leave it on your hair, and it prevents it from growing, so you never need a haircut. Or how about a formula for dog tails that makes them glow in the dark? You know, I had almost perfected that spaghetti glow."

Emma Brown was busy taking some oatmeal cookies out of the oven. They had only arrived

at the cottage that afternoon, but she couldn't let a day go by without baking some dessert.

"It's like I've always said, Nell, a person can do anything if she puts her mind to it." She smiled. "Why don't you invent all three? That way you could have a dog that eats Play-Doh whose hair never grows and whose tail glows in the dark. I'm sure no one has ever thought of that." She laughed. "No one but my Nelly."

Nelly grinned. She loved the way her grandmother called her "my Nelly." The air in the cottage was warm and cozy with the scent of oatmeal cookies fresh from the oven. Nelly loved the way her grandmother could turn an ordinary day into something special with her homemade cakes and cookies.

"I'm glad we are in Seaview together, Grandma," Nelly said, biting into her cookie. She reached over to give Rugbee a piece. He was sound asleep under a chair, a heap of reddish brown fur snoring heavily. Even asleep, Rugbee looked sad. He was the saddest-looking dog Nelly had ever seen. There was something sad about his eyes. When he smiled he looked like he was about to cry.

"Was Rugbee always so sad-looking, Grandma?" Nelly asked, leaving a piece of cookie under Rugbee's nose.

"Well, no, it's just that he's so old," Emma Brown told her. "When he was a pup, he didn't have that sad look. You were a pretty happy fellow, weren't you, Rugbee?" Her grandmother smiled faintly as she lowered herself into the rocking chair by the fireplace. Her whole body sagged. Suddenly she seemed so old that Nelly had to look away.

"Having you around helps me remember what it was like to be young," Emma Brown sighed.

"What was it like when you were my age?" Nelly asked, looking into her grandmother's clear blue eyes.

"Well, it was quieter. We didn't have jets overhead and TVs and radios everywhere. I think I had some of the happiest moments of my life, back then," Emma Brown said wistfully. "I can remember a game we played in the ocean. It was just a silly little game, but I can still remember how good it made me feel. I was just about your age. My sister and I would lie down at the water's edge and pretend we were shells. We'd just lie there and let the waves take us wherever they pleased. We would let our bodies go limp and let the ocean carry us in and out and back and forth to the shore. My body felt so free then, with no

aches or pains. I remember how wonderful it
felt to be alive, with the sun on my skin and
the waves washing me up onto the beach. Oh,
I'd give anything to do that again, to be that
free." Her voice trailed off, as the rocker
creaked back and forth.

"Why can't you play shells now, Grandma?"
Nelly asked, sitting down beside the rocker.

"That's a game I've gotten too old to play."
Emma Brown sighed. "But it's a funny thing.
Even though my body's gotten old, there is a
part of me inside that is still very young. Sometimes when I watch children jumping rope or
running in the park, I close my eyes and feel
myself running with the wind in my hair. I can
feel the rope at my heels as I skip over it. A
part of you never gets old, I guess. Somewhere
inside of me is a little girl, just about your
age." She smiled down at Nelly.

Nelly didn't smile back. She was lost in
thought. I don't want Grandma to get any
older, she was thinking, as she looked out the
window to the beach. Why do people have to
get older? Why do they have to change? Suddenly, she remembered her grandmother's
words. "A person can do anything if she puts
her mind to it." If that were true, why couldn't
Nelly invent a formula that would make her

grandmother young again? All I have to do is put my mind to it, Nelly mumbled to herself.

As Emma Brown sat quietly rocking by the fireplace, Nelly went over to the window and pressed her nose against it. It was too dark to see the line of beach that stretched out just beyond the cottage's tiny yard, but as she stood there, an image rose up before her. She could see the ocean, its blue waves lapping over the smooth white sand. And she could see two little girls down at the water's edge. They were lying side by side and laughing above the roar of the waves.

Chapter 3

The quiet of the cottage was suddenly shattered by a loud rumble of thunder as drops of rain splashed down on the shingled roof.

"Well, Miss Scientist, it looks like we're in for a storm," Emma Brown said, rising from her chair. "I don't like the way these lights are dimming. Could you do a little investigating in the cellar and see if you can find some candles? The real estate man said that the owners keep candles down there in case the power goes out."

"Sure, Grandma." Nelly jumped up and opened the door leading to the cellar. She switched on the light and made her way down the narrow staircase. She quickly found the candles on the shelf. They were sitting on top of some old boxes of games and toys.

"Hey, Grandma," Nelly called up the stairs, "I found some old games and stuff down here. May I bring them up?"

"Yes, just be careful coming up those steps," her grandmother cautioned.

When Nelly reached the kitchen, she put the candles and the dusty boxes on the table. Emma Brown stood surveying the cluttered kitchen. "I'm beginning to understand what your mother means about your being so messy!" She shook her head, stepping over a box of chemicals. "You know, some of these toys from the basement look like antiques," she said, holding up an old checkerboard.

"Whose toys are they?" Nelly wanted to know.

"The owners', I suppose. These cottages have been rented out for years, and the owners keep certain things on hand for the renters. Candles for a storm and toys and games for rainy days."

"Oh, wow! Look at this!" Nelly burst out. "It's a chemistry set! An antique chemistry set!"

A loud crack of lightning snapped outside the door and the lights dimmed for a second. Then everything went black. Nelly's grandmother made her way to the counter and found the pack of matches she had used to light the oven.

"We have candles, now all we need are some candle holders," she said, lighting one of the candles.

Being a scientist at heart, Nelly loved solving problems. Within minutes she had come up with a solution. Dipping into her box of glassware, she brought out a rack of six test tubes and set it on the kitchen table. She placed a candle in each tube and lit them all.

"Science to the rescue," Nelly said, as the flickering candlelight made the kitchen glow. She looked down at the table and ran her fingers across the top of the chemistry set, leaving a trail in the dust. The deep-red letters were edged in gold leaf. Nelly had never seen a chemistry set that had such fancy script. With a napkin, she wiped off the top of the box. It was like no chemistry set she had ever owned.

Nelly's other sets looked pretty much the same. The boxes all had ordinary type on them, and an ordinary picture of a smiling boy or girl holding up a test tube.

This set was different. There was nothing ordinary about it. A picture of a wizard holding up an unusual fluted glass bottle was on top.

The bottle looked like an ancient glass beaker and was filled with a sparkling blue-green potion. The wizard was dressed in a robe of deep purple, flecked with hundreds of shimmering gold stars. As Nelly looked closer, the stars seemed to give off a light of their own against the swirls of rich purple cloth. Then Nelly noticed the wizard's eyes. She had never seen such eyes. They were cobalt blue edged by the silvery white of the wizard's bushy eyebrows. She followed the direction of his eyes to the beaker in his hand. Suddenly, an iridescent mist seemed to rise from the glass and engulf him!

Nelly stood transfixed, not sure if what she was seeing was a picture or something real. In the flickering glow of the candlelight, she read the words that were just above the wizard's head:

McFINNEY'S POWERFUL POTIONS
A CHEMISTRY SET FOR
BOYS AND GIRLS
WHO DARE TO DREAM

"Nelly, Nelly Brown, do you hear me?"
Nelly blinked and looked up abruptly. Her grandmother was blowing out the candles.

"Come on, hon. You can play with these things all day tomorrow. It's getting late, and the candles won't last much longer. Let's get ready for bed." Emma Brown picked up a candle and carried it into the bedroom.

"OK, Grandma, just let me look inside." But when Nelly tried to open the chemistry set, she found that it was locked.

I never knew there were sets that locked, she mumbled to herself. She picked up the box and looked underneath it for a key, but there wasn't one. It must be in the cellar, she thought.

"Grandma, may I go down into the cellar just once more?" Nelly called into the bedroom.

"Not tonight, Nell. You can go down tomorrow, when it's light. I don't want you wandering around there in the dark. Bring that last candle with you and come to bed."

Nelly didn't argue. As much as she wanted to find the key, she was feeling a little frightened. She couldn't tell exactly why. Was it the storm and the candlelight or the funny feeling she got from looking at the antique chemistry set? As she picked up the candle from the test tube, she was drawn once more to the old box. When her eyes rested on the wizard, she let out a gasp that almost blew out the candle.

A shiver raced from her neck down to the backs of her bare arms as she stood staring at the box. This time it wasn't the wizard's robe or his eyes that caught her attention. It was the sight of his outstretched palm. Why hadn't she noticed it before? She was almost sure that it hadn't been open like that. It was stretched out toward her, with two delicate seashells in the palm. Her eyes were pulled back to the fancy script and in the light of her wobbly candle, she whispered the words: "FOR BOYS AND GIRLS WHO DARE TO DREAM."

That night, as the wind blew the rain against the windows of the little gray cottage, Nelly Brown lay dreaming. Her dreams were filled with potions and mists and the echo of the waves washing seashells back and forth upon the sand.

Chapter 4

Nelly awoke the next morning to the aroma of cinnamon muffins and the sound of her grandmother's humming in the kitchen. The fear and uneasiness that she had experienced the night before were gone, blown out to sea with the evening's storm. Dressing in the bright morning sunlight, Nelly was eager to take another look at the chemistry set and find the key to unlock it.

"Grandma, what happened to all the old toys from the cellar?" she cried, when she went into the kitchen and saw that the table was bare. For a minute she wondered if the wizard and starry robe had been part of a dream.

"Don't worry, I put everything on that little counter by the refrigerator," her grandmother said, setting a glass of orange juice on the table.

Nelly smiled when she saw the old multi-colored box with the fancy letters. The wizard was just as he had been the night before. So, it wasn't a dream, Nelly thought to herself, walking toward the cellar door. Now, all I have to do is find the key.

"Are you going to walk past a plate of your grandmother's cinnamon muffins without so much as a nibble?" Emma Brown called from the sink. "You have the rest of the summer to go rooting around in the cellar. Come and have your breakfast while the muffins are still warm."

Nelly let out a loud sigh and sank onto a kitchen chair. She felt she was on the brink of something really wonderful. She just "knew it in her bones," as her grandmother would say. All she had to do was find the key, a key that would unlock the secrets of McFinney's Powerful Potions, secrets that only a real scientist could unravel. But first she had to sit like a good little girl and eat her muffins.

"Do you think Madame Curie's grand-mother made her eat muffins when she was on the brink of her biggest discovery?" Nelly mumbled through a mouthful of muffin.

"Definitely," Emma Brown replied. "Behind all your greatest scientists, you'll find a grandmother making them eat their muffins. It's a well-known fact," she quipped.

They both started to laugh, when suddenly the glass of orange juice in Emma Brown's hand slipped and fell over on the table.

"Good grief! Now there's juice all over everything! Nelly, quick, get a wet dishrag from the sink."

Nelly sprang up and got a dishrag for the table. Her grandmother quickly began mopping up the spill. Nelly stood watching her grandmother's twisted fingers as they grasped the rag and ran it back and forth.

"My arthritis is always worse in the morning." Emma Brown sighed. "And with that rainy weather yesterday, well, never mind. The sun is finally shining, and we can spend some time outside. The fresh air will do us both good."

"Sure, Grandma, just let me look in the cellar for a while. I need to find the key to that old chemistry set," Nelly told her. She opened the cellar door and made her way down the steps. Running her hand over the shelf where the old toys had been, Nelly stopped and looked down at her smooth, straight fingers.

Will they get twisted and bent someday like Grandma's? she wondered. She couldn't imagine her smooth skin ever getting that wrinkly and stiff. Why do people have to get old? What would happen to her grandmother if she got even older? Nelly winced at the thought and turned her attention back to finding the key. But after twenty minutes of looking in every nook and cranny of the little cellar, she still had not found it.

She decided to take a break and set up her lab. She could finish searching for the key later on. But when she went into the kitchen and gazed at the little counter piled high with boxes, her heart sank.

"Why such a long face?" her grandmother asked, as she stood at the sink washing dishes.

"I can't find the key to the old chemistry set and even if I could, this space is just too small for experiments." Nelly looked out the kitchen window into the backyard. Suddenly she had an idea.

"Grandma, how about the little shed outside? Could I set up my lab in there?"

"You'll have to see what's inside first," her grandmother replied.

"I looked around the shed yesterday," Nelly told her. "It's almost empty. There's just some sand toys and rafts and stuff inside. I know I could make it into a great laboratory."

"Well, I don't see why not." Her grandmother smiled. "You can even have that little table on the porch, if there's room for it."

"I'll make room." Nelly was out the door and grabbing the little table before her grandmother could say another word. When she got to the shed, she undid the door latch. The gray weathered boards creaked as Nelly pulled the door open. She smiled, looking around. It was perfect. It was just big enough for one person, two if she took out the beach chairs and rafts. There were some shovels, a boat oar, and a paddle leaning against one wall. On the other wall, there was a small window and an old raft. Nelly was glad because she could close the door and still have light.

There was a small overgrown garden next to the shed that her grandmother had decided to restore for the summer. Nelly picked up the rake and shovel and took them outside to Emma Brown, who had come out to look at the garden.

"It's not quite a laboratory yet," her grandmother said, peeking into the shed. "And this isn't quite a garden yet," she sighed, looking at the little patch of weeds next to the shed. "We

have our work cut out for us this morning."
Emma Brown picked up the shovel and began
turning over the soil. "You know, Nell, you
can put all that stuff from the shed into the
cellar, as long as you remember to put it back
when we leave at the end of the summer."

Nelly spent the rest of the morning moving
things around and making trips back and forth
to the cellar. She found some old shelf paper
and tacked it to the wall. Then she nailed a
string next to it and tied a marking pen to the
end of the string. She drew some lines on the
paper and numbered them. Now she had a
graph sheet to plot out the progress of her
experiments.

For some reason, Rugbee fell in love with
the lab. Nelly's grandmother thought it was
because he loved small places, but Nelly knew
it was because Rugbee shared her love of science. He also shared her love of oatmeal cookies, so she kept some crumbs in a corner for
him.

Nelly looked around at the old shed, smiling
at its transformation. On the ledge under the
window, she had set up her test tube rack, and
on the shelves next to them, she had placed all
her bottles of chemicals. She had put her beakers, stirrers, and litmus paper on the table,

and the old chemistry set on an upturned milk crate.

"Well, Rugbee, old boy, we did it. It really looks like a laboratory." Nelly smiled. "Except for those sand pails in the corner. I'll have to put them in the cellar with the other junk."

That's when she noticed the old pail. It was sitting in the corner with the other sand pails, but somehow it stood out. It seemed to be giving off some kind of light. Holding it up, Nelly realized that the gold stars that were painted all over it actually glittered against the purple background. Nelly suddenly recognized the design. It was the same as the one on the wizard's robe, only delicately painted seashells were entwined among the stars. The bucket must be connected in some way to the old chemistry set!

Nelly looked inside, and a shiver of excitement ran through her. There at the bottom of the bucket lay a little tarnished key.

It must be the key to the chemistry set! As Nelly looked again at the shimmering stars on the old chipped bucket, she knew that she had been meant to find the key and unlock the secrets of McFinney's Powerful Potions. She also knew that most kids probably would never have found the key, or if they had, they wouldn't have known how to use the set. They would have just fooled around with it. But Nelly Brown had more serious intentions. Standing in her laboratory, she made a decision.

Forget the edible Play-Doh, she thought. Anybody can invent that. No, I will invent a formula that's much more challenging. I will invent a formula that will stop my grandmother from getting any older! It will be a formula that will let her grow younger!

Nelly felt an eerie confidence as she squeezed the key in her hand and walked over to the old chemistry set. She could feel her eyes being pulled back to the wizard's gaze as she listened to the faint humming of her grandmother working outside in the garden.

Chapter 5

Nelly had just picked up the old chemistry set and put it on the little table. She was about to try the key in the lock when she heard the phone ringing in the cottage. It was probably a call from her parents. She wanted to talk to them, but not especially now.

"Nelly, run and answer that, will you? With these old legs, I'll never get there in time," called her grandmother.

Nelly reluctantly put down the key and hurried outdoors. When she got inside the cottage, she stopped. For a minute she forgot where the phone was. She ran into the kitchen and then into the living room. She finally found the phone and answered with a breathless "Hello."

"Nelly? Is that you?" a familiar voice asked.

At first Nelly didn't know who it was and then she realized that it was her aunt Marie.

"How are you, Nelly?"

"Fine."

"How's Grandma?"

"Fine."

"Are you having a good time?"

"Yes."

"How's the weather?"

"Fine."

Nelly was definitely not in the mood to make conversation with an ordinary grown-up. Luckily, her cousin Ben came on the line just then.

"Hey, Nell, how's it going?"

"Hi, Ben! It's going great. We had this storm last night and I found this old chemistry set and I made this neat lab. . . ." Nelly was talking so fast that her words ran into one another. She could hear Ben's froggy laughter on the other end.

"Slow down, slow down. You can tell me all about it when I see you next week," he broke in.

"Next week? What are you talking about?" Nelly didn't understand.

"You know how I usually spend the summer with my dad and stepmom? Well, they have to go to New Mexico for two weeks, and since my mom has already made plans to start some courses at college, she's going to ask Grandma if I can stay with you guys for those two weeks," Ben explained.

"Whoooopeeee!" Nelly let out such a loud whoop that it brought her grandmother running into the cottage.

"What's all the excitement about?" she asked.

Nelly handed her the phone. For a moment she forgot all about the chemistry set. All she could think of was her cousin's coming. Nelly smiled as she thought of Ben, with his clear blue eyes, just like their grandmother's, and just like her own, and his wavy red hair. He was a year older than Nelly and they looked so much alike, they often pretended to be brother and sister in front of strangers. They were both only children and so had always been close, but their friendship was based on something more. They understood one another.

"We're allies," Ben explained to her once. "Anybody can have a cousin, but we are bound by more than blood. Our very souls are entwined."

Nelly had giggled and rolled her eyes. When Ben's parents had divorced, they had felt so sorry for him that they'd bought him a television set for his bedroom. Nelly could always tell when Ben had stayed up late watching old movies. He'd show up the next day with deep circles under his eyes and would talk about "entwined souls." Only Ben could come up with something like that. He didn't watch MTV like normal kids. He wasn't like anyone else Nelly knew. That's what made him so special.

And now he was coming for two whole weeks! Nelly couldn't wait to show him her lab and the old chemistry set. The chemistry set! She had forgotten all about it. Opening her hand she looked down at the little key. Should she wait for Ben? She could imagine the two of them opening the set together, but did she really want to wait a whole week? She closed her fingers over the key and raced past her grandmother, who was still on the phone.

Once inside her lab, Nelly shut the door and ran over to the old chemistry set. She fixed her eyes on the wizard's stare and put the key in the lock. Her heart pounded in her ears. Would it fit? Would it really open the set? What would she find? In a second, her questions were answered. The key easily slipped into the lock. Nelly quickly turned it and opened the box. It was better than she could have imagined. If a chemistry set could be described as glorious, then this was one glorious chemistry set!

The inside of the box was lined in deep blue velvet. Little bottles of the strangest shapes, each containing the most extraordinary colored powders that Nelly had ever seen, were lined up on the left. They were held in place by a fancy framework of brass that was latched to the side of the box.

A beautiful fluted glass beaker, like the one the wizard was holding on the cover, stood in a panel on the right side. A set of test tubes of various lengths stood above it and next to them was some intricate glass tubing, swirls of blue and green glass. A leather-bound book, covered in purple velvet, was in another panel. There were no words on the cover, just a sprinkling of gold-threaded stars that formed a delicate spiral, like the shape of a snail shell.

Nelly sat down at the rickety little table and ran her fingers over the lush velvet cover of the book. Tracing the spiral of stars with her index finger, she began to tremble. She had stumbled onto something far out of the ordi-

nary, something very rare and wonderful and frightening.

Nelly opened the book and read the words at the top of page one.

"Welcome, dreamer, child of the universe . . ."

Chapter 6

"**M**cFinney's Powerful Potions have been formulated just for you." Nelly smiled to herself. She already knew that. She read on.

"The stuff of your dreams is within your reach. With these ancient extracts and compounds, mixed and blended in the correct measurements, you will be able to see the impossible become possible before your very eyes! This chemistry set is equipped to perform but one experiment per person. Simply follow the instructions on page two. Caution: Be sure to choose your experiment with care for it is guaranteed to succeed. This set is recommended for dreamers over the age of six years."

"I knew it," Nelly mumbled aloud. "I just knew this set was special." She turned to page two.

"Once you have decided on your experiment, write your name and age in the ledger at the back of the book. Under your name describe the formula you seek to create. The instructions for making it will automatically appear on page three." Nelly quickly paged through to the back of the book. When she got to the ledger she was surprised to find a long list of the names and the formulas of those who had gone before her.

Many of the names were written in strange letters and symbols that Nelly couldn't understand. She skipped over these and began to read some of the writing that she *could* make out.

67. Gowen Ashland, age fifteen years. I seek a love potion formula for the fair Lady Ann, a potion that will fill her heart with love for me and no other.

82. Gareth McGrath, age nine years. I seek a formula that will turn potatoes into gold.

91. Belinda Mosley, age ten years. I seek a formula that will make my father invisible so the redcoats won't be able to see him.

106. Emily Woodring, age eight years. I seek a formula that will turn all the dust of this prairie into bluebells, just as blue as those back home in Virginia.

111. Avery Kaufmann, age ten years. I seek a formula that will make horses fly so that people can ride them over the ocean.

120. Martin Perterson, age eleven years. I seek a formula that will turn all the leaves on our apple tree into hundred-dollar bills.

124. Amy Cohen, age nine years. I seek a formula that will turn my brother into the donkey that he really is.

125. Angela Piloti, age eight years. I seek a formula that will rid the earth of oatmeal forever.

Nelly looked down at the last number on the list.

211. Daniel Reece, age seven years. I seek a formula to make the mustache on my math teacher, Miss Unger, turn green.

Nelly untied the marker next to her graph sheet. Next to number 212 in the ledger, she wrote: "Nelly Brown, age ten years. I seek a formula that will stop my grandmother from getting older and make her younger instead."

She went back to page three and read the instructions carefully.

"The formula you seek is made up of one equal part of Binazar and Celizar and two equal parts of Finazar. You can make these ancient compounds from the rare mineral powders in this set. Filter each compound with a quarter of a liter of rainwater and two drops of seawater. The proper measurements are given below for the compounds. Once you have mixed and filtered them, add them to two parts of rainwater in the large beaker. Stir and let everything sit overnight. This formula is not to be taken internally. Do not let anyone drink it. It is for external use only."

Nelly spent the rest of the afternoon in her lab mixing powders. Then she searched the yard for some rainwater. She finally found some in an old washtub on the side of the cottage. To get seawater, she took the old sand bucket and raced down to the beach. By the time her grandmother called Nelly in for supper, she had just added the last compound, Finazar, to the large beaker. With a glass stirrer she swirled the blue-green potion until it bubbled to the top. Then she watched as it began to change colors from blue-green to deep purple, and finally to bright orange.

When Nelly heard her grandmother calling again, she wanted to yell at her to come see the bubbling formula. But she decided to surprise her grandmother instead. She wouldn't say a word about the formula. She'd just wait and try it out on her grandmother in the morning.

Nelly gulped her supper as fast as she could, then rushed back out to her lab. The formula had changed colors again. It was now a glowing yellow, filled with swirls of pink. Nelly sat at the little table, her eyes riveted to the beaker. It was by far the most beautiful potion that she had ever made and she couldn't wait to try it out.

But as she sat staring at the still bubbling potion, Nelly wrinkled her nose. If she couldn't let her grandmother drink the formula, how could she get it to work?

Nelly reached for the instruction book and read through it again, but she couldn't find an answer to her question.

"For external use only." Nelly read the words aloud. Somehow, she would have to get the formula *on* her grandmother, but how? Her thoughts were suddenly interrupted by Emma Brown, who was knocking on the laboratory door. Nelly sprang to her feet and opened the door a crack. She poked her head out.

"My goodness, there must be some fantastic experimenting going on in here," her grandmother said, reaching for the door handle. "How about letting me have a look?"

"Not yet, not yet," Nelly cried, holding the

door as close to her as she could. "It's a surprise, Grandma. I'll show it to you tomorrow, I promise."

"I suppose I can wait, but you really have me wondering. Is it the edible Play-Doh or the hair stunting shampoo? Speaking of shampoo, it's time we washed our hair. We can use that big old sink in the kitchen. I can help you with yours and you can help me with mine."

That's it! That's it, Nelly thought to herself. "Uh, do you think we could wait until tomorrow morning? I was hoping we could go for a walk on the beach and look for shells," Nelly said hopefully. What she really wanted to do was stay right where she was, watching her formula, but she knew she'd better do something to distract her grandmother. If they could wash their hair tomorrow morning, Nelly could wash the formula into her grandmother's hair!

That evening they walked along the beach. The blue-green waves reflected the light from the setting sun. As Nelly looked at her grandmother, who was searching for shells, she thought about how things soon would be different, very different. She stood, trying to fix Emma Brown in her memory. She wanted to remember her as she was in her faded pink

sweatshirt and baggy white pants with the cuffs rolled up. Her grandmother was smiling, her silvery curls framing her face beneath her floppy straw hat. Nelly knew that she would remember that smile, since she had known it all her life. It had always been there for her.

"Oh, Nell, come and look at this one. It's a real beauty," her grandmother called as she held up a shell.

Nelly walked up beside her, and together they stood in that special light that bounces off the sea at sunset, bathing everything in gold. Nelly held out her bucket as her grandmother dropped in the shell. Together they walked along the water's edge, picking up more shells, until Nelly's bucket was full. She swung it gently back and forth as they came up the lane to the cottage. Her treasures of shells and sea glass rattled on the bottom, making a kind of music, while the little gold stars on the outside of the old chipped bucket shimmered in the twilight.

Chapter 7

"The formula!" It was the first thing that Nelly thought of when she opened her eyes the next morning. She was so excited that she yelled it out.

"What did you say?" Emma Brown called from the bedroom where she was dressing.

"Oh, . . . French toast. I said French toast sure would taste good this morning," Nelly answered, racing past her grandmother's room and into the bathroom. While standing at the sink getting a drink of water, Nelly noticed another glass with her grandmother's false teeth floating in it. Nelly couldn't resist. She stuck her finger in the glass to see if the teeth would bite. They didn't. She quickly took her finger out when she heard her grandmother coming out of her bedroom. She wanted to get to the lab before her grandmother made her eat breakfast.

"French toast it is. But slow down. I thought we were going to wash our hair this morning," Emma Brown said, following Nelly into the kitchen.

"We are, we are, but can't we eat first? I'm starved." Nelly had edged her way to the door.

"I see. Well, do you mind telling me just where you're off to in such a state of hunger?"

"I have to check up on some things in my lab. Could you call me when the French toast is ready?" Nelly didn't wait for a reply. She hurried to the backyard and quickly undid the latch on the door of the shed, stepping inside.

The old beaker stood on the little table, just as it had all night long, only now the formula was completely clear. Nelly gave it a stir but it remained unchanged. She put her nose down and smelled it but there was no scent. Would the formula really work? Was McFinney's Powerful Potions a real chemistry set or just a toy with a lot of colored powders?

No, Nelly knew it was special. If the formula had changed to a liquid that looked like water, then there was a reason for it. Nelly smiled. Of course! She wouldn't be able to pour it on her grandmother's head if it were a funny color or had a funny smell. This was just right. This was perfect!

Nelly set the formula on the porch just outside the screen door to the kitchen. Then she ran inside, where she found Emma Brown at the stove.

"May we wash our hair now, Grandma? Mine is really dirty. It's so dirty it almost hurts," she said, leaning against the sink.

Emma Brown laughed. "Now, that's what I call dirty! We'll get you fixed up right after breakfast. Sit down and have your French toast."

But Nelly was too excited to eat. She just poked at the toast with her fork.

"I thought you said you were starved!" her grandmother said, noticing Nelly's untouched food.

"I was, but my hair is so dirty I can't eat."

"Now I've heard everything!" Emma Brown sighed. "Just try and imagine how good you'll feel after we wash it. Hurry up and eat your breakfast!"

Nelly began shoveling the French toast into her mouth. In a flash she was up and washing her plate at the sink.

Her grandmother shook her head. "One minute you're starved and the next you're not and the next you devour everything on your plate in the blink of an eye! And now you're actually going to wash your dish? We both know how you hate washing dishes. Do you mind telling me what brings all this on?"

"I'm just trying to help out, Grandma. Come on, I'll wash your hair first."

"Oh, no, if your hair is so dirty that it hurts, we'll take care of it right now," her grandmother insisted. "Here, stand on this chair."

Nelly impatiently climbed on the chair, taking little notice of Rugbee, who had decided to curl up and have his nap beneath it. Nelly bent over and put her head under the faucet. It seemed to take hours for her grandmother to wash her hair. She wasn't satisfied with just washing it once. She washed it three times!

Finally, with her hair in a towel, Nelly jumped off the chair and tried moving it to the side of the sink. Rugbee groaned, and Nelly had to nudge him with her foot to get him to move. As Emma Brown bent over, Nelly turned on the water and began rubbing her fingers through her grandmother's hair.

"Wait a minute, Grandma, this shampoo bottle is almost empty. I'll get another one from the bathroom. You just keep getting your hair wet while I'm gone."

Nelly made a dash for the bathroom, grabbed a new bottle of shampoo, and raced back to the kitchen. Then she quietly opened the screen door and reached for the beaker of formula.

"OK, Grandma, here's the shampoo. Keep your eyes closed," Nelly told her grandmother, working the shampoo into her hair. After she had gotten up a good lather, she turned the water back on and began to rinse it.

"Oh, that feels wonderful," Emma Brown sighed, as Nelly ran her fingers over her grandmother's scalp.

"Pretty soon you're going to feel really wonderful," Nelly said, reaching for the beaker. "Keep your eyes closed, Grandma. There's still some soap that I have to get out. OK, here goes."

As she began pouring the formula over her grandmother's head, Rugbee suddenly sat up. Nelly and the chair went toppling over. Fortunately Nelly was able to hold onto the beaker and keep it from breaking. Unfortunately, she wasn't able to keep it from tipping over. The last quarter of the formula spilled out onto the kitchen floor. Nelly knew that most of it had landed on her grandmother's hair but she was horrified to discover Rugbee licking up

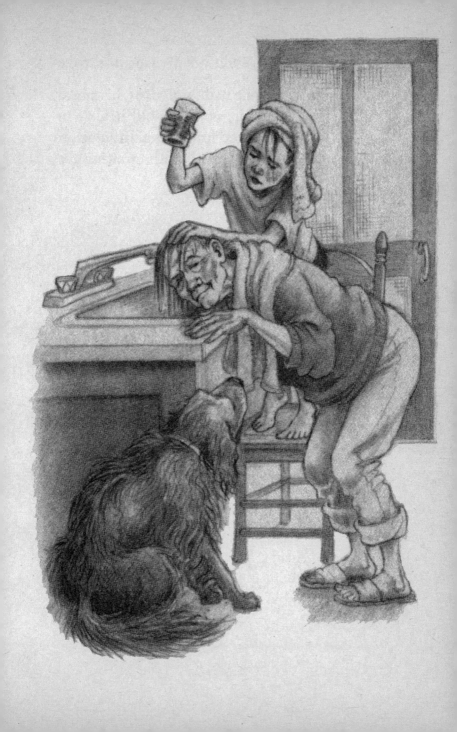

the little puddle that had landed by his nose!

Sitting on the floor, with the old beaker in her hands, Nelly looked from her grandmother to Rugbee. She held her breath, waiting for one of them to change.

Chapter 8

"Are you all right?" Emma Brown asked, lifting her head out of the sink.

"I'm OK. How do you feel, Grandma?" Nelly was still sitting on the floor. She was staring up at her grandmother.

"Well, I'm fine, but I'm not the one who just went flying off a chair." Emma Brown laughed. "Oh, hon, what are you doing with that beaker? You could have really hurt yourself if that had broken. I think you should keep all your glass equipment in your lab."

Nelly frowned. Her grandmother sounded the same. She looked the same too. Her face was still wrinkly and worn-looking. Her hair was still gray.

"Don't you feel a little different?" Nelly asked, standing up.

"Why should I feel different? You didn't sneak any secret potions into my orange juice this morning, did you?" Her grandmother smiled, as she picked up the chair and put it back at the table.

"No, it's just . . . well, being at the ocean and all, I thought it would make you feel different, better, you know?" Nelly searched her grandmother's face for signs of change.

"Now that you mention it, I think I do feel different," Emma Brown admitted as she dried her hair.

"You do? How?"

"I'm not the same as I was a few minutes ago. I'm definitely different."

"Really? How? How different?" Nelly was having a hard time concealing her excitement.

"Well, my hair used to be dirty and now it's clean. Isn't that amazing?" Emma Brown laughed.

Nelly groaned and looked at Rugbee. He looked exactly the same, too; sleepy, sad-looking, and old, even after licking up the formula. The book had said that it was not to be taken internally. Nelly hoped that since he was a dog he would be all right, but she was also hoping for some change.

She looked at her grandmother and then at

Rugbee again. No one had changed at all!
Nelly was so disappointed that she wanted to
throw the old beaker in the garbage can. Then
she remembered that the chemistry set didn't
belong to her. It went with the cottage.

That's OK, she thought. I'll put it back in
the box so that next year some other kid can
find it and get gypped like me. She was angry.
She had really believed in McFinney's Powerful Potions.

Nelly couldn't shake her feeling of disappointment for the rest of the day. She decided
to stay out of her lab and go to the beach with
her grandmother. But even the ocean couldn't
cheer her up. That night, before going to bed,
she bent down to have one more look at Rugbee. He was snoring loudly under the coffee
table in the living room.

"Rugbee, you'll never change. All you ever
do is sleep." Nelly sighed, scratching his head.

"If you were his age, you'd be doing the
same thing," her grandmother said, looking up
from her newspaper. "In fact, I think we could
all use some extra sleep after so much sun
today. What do you say we turn in early?"

Nelly didn't object. It had been a long day.
One of the most disappointing days of her life!
It had been like Christmas with no presents.

This was the worst part of being a scientist. She tried to imagine how her favorite scientist would have acted. What would Madame Curie have done with McFinney's Powerful Potions? McFinney's Powerful Duds is more like it, she thought gloomily.

Nelly had seen a picture of Madame Curie in her science book at school. She was wearing a long black dress with a white apron. Her hair was light and curly and piled in a bun. Madame Curie looked smart and serious. Nelly hoped that she would grow up to look the same way.

That night, Nelly dreamed that she was in a wonderful laboratory. She was wearing a long black dress with a white apron. Her curly brown hair was piled on her head, just like Madame Curie's. She felt smart and serious. People were calling her Madame Nelly! She was standing at a lab table pouring a bright blue liquid from one test tube to another. Suddenly Rugbee walked in, but he looked different. His hair was very short and his tail was glowing. When he came up to Nelly he spit a piece of Play-Doh out on her shoe! He started to bark, which was unusual for Rugbee, since he was usually too lazy to bark. In fact the barking grew louder and louder. That's when Nelly woke up.

She blinked her eyes and realized that she had been dreaming. She blinked again. Yes, she was awake all right, but why did she still hear Rugbee barking? Since when did Rugbee have enough energy to bark that much? Nelly climbed out of bed and sleepily walked into the kitchen to investigate. When she got there, her eyes opened wide in amazement.

I must still be dreaming, she mumbled under her breath, for there at the kitchen sink, in her grandmother's pink sweatshirt and baggy white pants, was a beautiful redheaded woman of about thirty! A frisky young dog was barking at her side.

"It can't be!" Nelly stammered. "It just can't be!" The woman turned and smiled at her. As Nelly looked into her clear blue eyes, she realized that she was looking into the eyes of Emma Brown!

"Good grief, Grandma . . . is that you?"

Chapter 9

"Of course it's me," the beautiful woman said, laughing. Nelly shivered. It was her grandmother's laugh, only it was lighter and not so crackly.

Nelly couldn't move. She stood in the doorway, gaping. Suddenly she thought of Little Red Riding Hood and the line, "But, Grandma, what big teeth you have!" only Nelly was thinking, But Grandma, what real teeth you have! Emma Brown was now much too young and much too beautiful to keep her teeth in a glass on the sink!

Nelly had never imagined that her grandmother was once so beautiful, yet here she stood, her once silver hair now a luxurious red! It looked as soft and bouncy as the hair on shampoo commercials. Her eyes were the same blue as always, but there was no redness around them. And her skin; Emma Brown's skin was so smooth that there wasn't a wrinkle on her face and it seemed to glow a soft peachy color. She brushed her hair back with hands that were now straight and beautiful, not twisted and full of brown spots, as they had been.

"I've made a nice cranberry nut loaf for breakfast," Emma Brown said, her voice clear and energetic. "And when we're through, we'll take Rugbee to the beach for his run." Run? Rugbee, run? Nelly never had seen her grandmother's sleepy old dog run. But looking down at Rugbee, she realized that there was nothing sleepy or old about him. Now his coat was shiny and his eyes sparkled. His body was lean and not so lumpy. He was full of energy and he didn't look sad anymore. He looked happy and frisky and glad to be alive.

Sitting down at the kitchen table, Nelly couldn't take her eyes off this new and improved Emma Brown. Only Nelly wasn't so sure that this was an improvement. She didn't like looking at a grandmother who was so young and pretty. She missed the way her grandmother used to look, the way all grandmothers are supposed to look, like they've been around for a long time. She found herself missing Emma Brown's crinkly wrinkles and silver hair. She didn't know if she could get used to this version.

"Have you looked in the mirror this morning, . . . Grandma?" Nelly had a hard time getting the "Grandma" out. She still felt like she was talking to a stranger.

"I did, and I saw my first gray hair! I think I'll stay away from mirrors from now on," said Emma Brown.

So that's how the formula works, Nelly thought. She doesn't realize that anything has changed. It's as if she always looked like this. Nelly wondered if she should tell her grandmother about the formula, but how could she convince someone so gorgeous that she was really an old woman, with not one gray hair but a whole head full? As Nelly sat and wondered what to do, the phone rang.

"I'll get it," Emma Brown said, sprinting into the living room.

Meanwhile, Nelly looked down at Rugbee. "I can't even call you 'good old Rugbee' anymore," she said, sighing. Staring at his happy perky face, Nelly realized that she missed his sad and sleepy look. She remembered the tired Rugbee, like an old lumpy pillow that you could curl up against and fall asleep. But this Rugbee, this younger Rugbee, didn't look like he did much sleeping at all.

Suddenly Emma Brown was calling from the living room. "Nell, come and talk to your parents. Hurry, they're calling long distance."

Her parents! Nelly had forgotten all about them! What would they say when they saw Grandma? Nelly wondered how her father would react to having a mother who was ten years younger than her son! She wondered if he could hear any difference in Emma Brown's voice. He could. It was the first thing that he mentioned when she picked up the phone.

"Hi, Nell. Your grandmother sounds wonderful. You two must really be having a good time!"

"Oh . . . yes . . . things are OK," Nelly managed to mumble.

"OK? Just *OK?* According to Grandma, everything is great. Speaking of great, you should see the phylum your mother and I have been collecting. This algae would knock your socks off, Nell. I heard about your lab. Have you come up with any new discoveries? Anything earthshaking?"

"Uh . . . well . . . I guess you could say I've come up with something like that," Nelly

croaked, as she looked at her grandmother doing knee bends in the doorway.

"It's Grandma," Nelly was finally able to
whisper into the phone, as her grandmother
walked into the kitchen.

"What about Grandma?" her father asked.

"You see, I found this old chemistry set and
I made up this potion for Grandma and now
. . . well she's . . . prettier."

"Nelly, you know what I've told you about
drinking your potions. You know that's very
dangerous!" Her father began his usual lec-
ture.

"No, Dad," Nelly interrupted, "I wouldn't
ever make a potion to drink. I poured this one
on her hair."

"What!" Her father yelled so loudly that
Nelly had to hold the phone away from her
ear. "Nelly Brown, I'm surprised at you! How
many times have I told you that people are not
guinea pigs? The chemicals you are using are
never to be used on people. Good grief! Is
your grandmother all right? Was her scalp
burned? You haven't turned her hair green or
anything, have you?"

"Well, no, not green exactly, it's more like
red," Nelly said weakly. At this she could hear

her father yell and drop the phone. She heard him calling to her mother.

"Nelly." It was the firm voice of her mother on the line now. "I'm very disappointed in you. I thought you were old enough to use that equipment in a responsible way. You simply can't endanger people like that. It's reckless and unscientific."

"But, Mom, you don't understand . . ."

"No, Nelly, you are the one who doesn't understand. If I find out that Grandma's hair or scalp is harmed in any way, we're going to have to take your chemistry set away from you until you've learned to be responsible enough to use it. Do I make myself clear?"

"Very." Nelly sighed.

"Good, now try and stay out of trouble. We miss you, Nell. Your father bought you a bag full of souvenirs from the Museum of Natural History. You know how he loves to buy souvenirs. Last night we went out for pizza. He wanted to wrap up a piece and send it to you, so that you could have a real piece of New York City pizza! I suggested some New York City jelly beans, instead. We'll be leaving for Virginia tomorrow. The work has been really interesting. Are you having a good time?"

"Uh, yes. . . . It's been pretty interesting here, too," Nelly said.

"I'm glad. Put Grandma back on and I'll talk to you soon. Bye, hon."

Nelly called her grandmother back to the phone and then flopped down on the couch.

"Oh, no, everything is fine," her grandmother was saying into the phone. "My hair? My hair has never looked better. Nelly can give a shampoo like a real pro. Damaged? Of course it isn't damaged. You two really do need a vacation. You're beginning to sound like two old worrywarts. Nelly and I are having a wonderful time. We both feel so good and so relaxed, why, you won't recognize us when you get back."

Oh, brother, Nelly moaned under her breath, there *is* one of us they won't recognize. And the other one had better come up with a potion to make herself invisible when they *do* show up!

Chapter 10

Nelly knew she'd be in big trouble if she couldn't figure out a way to get her grandmother back to normal. Otherwise, how could she ever explain the magic formula to her parents? She had to do something. She had to undo what the formula had done. But how? She went into her lab and sat down at the little table. With her head resting on her hands, she looked around until her eyes fell on the old chemistry set. That's when she remembered the instruction book.

"There's got to be something in here about undoing this stuff," she mumbled aloud, as she paged through the book. She read down to the bottom of page one and reread "Caution: Be sure to choose your experiment with care for it is guaranteed to succeed." It sure had! But there must be something about making things go back to normal.

Nelly read through the rest of the book but could find no mention of undoing the formula. She closed the book and put it back in the box. With shoulders sagging, she left the lab and went into the cottage to see what her grandmother was doing.

"I was just about to come and get you," Emma Brown said, as she sat on her bed brushing her beautiful red hair into a long braid down her back.

"Gosh, you're pretty," Nelly couldn't help but marvel.

Her grandmother smiled. "We come from a long line of good lookers and fast runners. Come on, Miss Brown, I'll race you to the beach." Before Nelly could blink, her grandmother had jumped off the bed and bolted for the door.

They spent the rest of the morning running along the beach and throwing pieces of driftwood for Rugbee to fetch. It took Nelly quite a while to get used to the fact that her grandmother could outrun her, but by the time they got back to the cottage for lunch, she was feeling a little better about things.

Maybe once her parents saw that Grandma

felt much better, they wouldn't be angry. Emma Brown was brimming over with good health. She was bubbly and full of energy and seemed to be laughing a lot. Nelly was beginning to think that things had worked out for the best, after all. Sure, she missed the way her grandmother used to look and sound, but now they could do things that they couldn't have done before.

They spent the next two days jogging and doing aerobics, and they even went to the amusement park in town. Grandma insisted they go on the roller coaster! Then they went shopping for matching bikini bathing suits!

It had been three days since Nelly had washed the formula into her grandmother's hair. As each day passed Emma Brown seemed to be feeling better and better. She was looking better, too, but by Wednesday, Nelly noticed something strange. Her grandmother was getting pimples! Nelly was at the breakfast table when she first saw them.

"What's on your face?" Nelly asked.

"Oh, you noticed! These zits, I hate them. Do they look too horrible? I'm not going to let anyone see me until they're all gone," Emma Brown cried, running into her bedroom and slamming the door.

She stayed there most of the day, polishing her fingernails and toenails. When Nelly went in to see what she was doing, she polished Nelly's fingernails and toenails, too. She even polished Rugbee's toenails, which made them all laugh, though Nelly didn't laugh for long. She was worried. Her grandmother was giggling a lot and acting silly.

While Emma Brown spent the day in her bedroom, Nelly tried working in the lab, but she couldn't concentrate. She kept running back and forth to check on her grandmother's condition, and it didn't seem to be getting any better.

Above the roar of the music blasting from her clock radio, Emma Brown told her granddaughter that she had seen "some real cute boys on the beach yesterday, awesomely cute, if you know what I mean." Nelly shook her head. Grandma was acting as goofy as Nelly's baby-sitter, Marty. She was beginning to look like Marty, too; sort of gangly, all arms and legs. Only Marty hadn't needed a special formula to look that way. She just looked that way because she was fifteen!

At six o'clock, Emma Brown made supper: peanut butter and jelly sandwiches with marshmallows for dessert. She even put a few

marshmallows in Rugbee's dish. He swallowed them in one gulp and ran into the living room. Nelly couldn't help noticing how much younger he looked; younger than he had looked yesterday! Her grandmother, meanwhile, was busy gazing at herself in the hall mirror.

"I think I'll get my nose pierced," she murmured. "And my hair! I hate my hair! I'm going to shave this half and dye the other half blue. What do you think?"

Oh, great! Mom and Dad will come back and find Grandma with pimples, half a head of blue hair, and an earring in her nose! I'm dead! Nelly moaned under her breath, getting up to clear the table. Emma Brown did not seem interested in doing the dishes. She had gotten her binoculars and was looking out the living room window at the beach.

Nelly remembered that her grandmother used to be an avid birdwatcher. "See any good ones?" Nelly called to her.

"Yeah, some cute ones, awesomely cute ones!"

"Yuck! Not that 'awesomely cute' junk again. I mean birds, not boys." Nelly shook her head in disgust. Then she looked down to see why her toes were suddenly wet.

She was standing on the edge of a puddle! A big yellow puddle! But where did it come from? Not Rugbee. It couldn't have been Rugbee. He had been housebroken since he was a pup. Nelly closed her eyes and groaned. She suddenly realized that if her grandmother had been growing younger in the last few days, so had Rugbee. And now he was so young, he wasn't even housebroken!

Nelly poked her head under the table to look for Rugbee, but instead of finding the old sleepy Rugbee or the young energetic Rugbee, she discovered a tiny little ball of fur. A puppy Rugbee! He wasn't even old enough to bark. He let out a little squeak when Nelly picked him up.

"Oh, my gosh!" Not only had the formula worked, but now it wouldn't stop. "Rugbee, look at you, you're just a baby! And if you're a baby, what's going to happen next to Grandma? What have I done?" Nelly whispered. "What have I done?"

Chapter 11

Rugbee's squeaky puppy cries kept Nelly up most of the night. She kept making trips back and forth to the kitchen, where she put him in a cardboard box. No sooner would she settle Rugbee down, than the loud music coming from her grandmother's bedroom radio would start him crying again. It seemed that Emma Brown had suddenly developed an appreciation for heavy metal music! Unfortunately, Rugbee didn't share her musical taste.

When Nelly finally opened her eyes the next morning, she was afraid to get out of bed. She closed them again, hoping that the last few days had been a bad dream and that her old grandmother would be back in the kitchen today, making muffins, with the big old sleepy Rugbee at her feet.

But there were no sounds coming from the kitchen. Instead, there was a great deal of noise coming from her grandmother's bedroom. Nelly opened her eyes wide and listened. She tried to figure out what was causing such a racket. It sounded like someone was jumping on a bed!

Nelly leaped up and ran down the hall to her grandmother's room. She threw open the door, expecting the worst. And that's just what she found, since on the bed, not sitting, but jumping, was Emma Brown. A little Emma Brown! A ten-year-old Emma Brown!

"Oh, my gosh!" Nelly groaned, as she watched the little redheaded girl in Grandma's nightgown, laughing and jumping on the bed. Emma Brown's pimples were gone, replaced by a sprinkling of freckles. Her red hair seemed redder and wilder with curls. She was just about Nelly's height, with skinny arms and legs. She looked at Nelly with a mischievous twinkle in her clear blue eyes.

Nelly had a sick feeling in her stomach. It was one thing to have her grandmother looking younger but it was too much having her look ten years old!

"Why, she's just . . . just . . . a kid! She's just like me, now!" Nelly sank down on the

chair beside the bed. She sat there a long time, trying to figure out what to do. Meanwhile, little Emma Brown kept jumping from one end of the bed to the other.

Nelly bit her lip and tried not to panic. She knew that Madame Curie would never panic if an experiment went wrong. Nelly wondered if any of Madame Curie's experiments ever turned out as wrong as this one. Nelly thought of the great scientist's face, so full of strength and confidence. All right, it was true, things looked pretty bad now, but they didn't have to stay this way. That's what science was all about, wasn't it? Solving problems and coming up with solutions. Somehow, she would find a solution. She had to believe that. She had to believe in herself, just the way Madame Curie did. Nelly thought again of her grandmother's advice. "A person can do anything if she puts her mind to it."

"That's it. I'm going back to my lab and I'm going to come up with a formula that will fix this," Nelly declared out loud. "As for you, Grandma, you know you aren't supposed to be jumping on the bed." Nelly tried to grab the baggy nightgown, but the little Emma Brown wouldn't stand still. "Hey, you're going to ruin the springs on this bed if you don't stop it,"

Nelly scolded. She was finally able to grab a leg and pull the laughing child down to the floor.

"I want to go swimming. Let's go swimming, Nell," Emma Brown said in her now girlish voice. She ran to the dresser and began to look for a bathing suit.

"Not now," Nelly told her. "I've got to work in my lab first, then we can go. Come into my room and I'll lend you one of my suits." They went into Nelly's bedroom, and Nelly found an extra bathing suit.

"I want to go swimming now," Emma Brown whined.

"Well, you'll just have to wait. I have some important stuff to do," Nelly said firmly. She handed her the bathing suit. "Here you go, er . . . Grandma . . . er . . . Emma." Nelly felt silly calling someone her own age Grandma.

"Emmy, just call me Emmy. That's what I like to be called." She was about to step out of the nightgown when she got that mischievous look back in her eye. "Can you do something for me?" she asked softly.

"Sure, what?" Nelly answered.

"Could you close your eyes while I change? It's because . . . because I have these five belly buttons, and I hate to have anyone staring at them." She lowered her eyes and put her hand over her stomach.

"Well, yeah. OK." Nelly closed her eyes. Five belly buttons! She never knew that her grandmother had five belly buttons! Why hadn't anyone told her before? Now that she thought of it, she couldn't remember ever seeing her grandmother's stomach. She heard Emmy getting changed and wondered what a stomach with five belly buttons looked like. She had to know. Nelly cracked one eye open to take a peek, just as Emmy was heading out the door!

"Hey, where are you going?" Nelly called after her.

"Me and my five belly buttons are going for a swim." Emmy Brown laughed as she raced for the beach.

"Why, that little liar!" Nelly stood in a daze. She couldn't get over the fact that her grandmother had told such a lie, then laughed when Nelly had believed the silly story about the five belly buttons. Nelly never imagined that her grandmother was that kind of kid. Actually, she'd never imagined her grandmother as a kid at all. She knew things would be different if Grandma got younger, but she never thought they would turn out like this.

Nelly quickly changed into her bathing suit and was about to run up to the beach, when she remembered Rugbee. What had become of Rugbee? If Grandma had gotten this young so fast, the effects of the formula must be accelerating. Nelly ran into the kitchen and groaned when she found the cardboard box empty.

"Here, Rugbee. Here, boy," she called as she searched the kitchen for the missing pup. When Nelly couldn't find him, she decided to run to the beach before she lost Grandma, too. Before she left, she got the box of doggy treats down from the cabinet and put one in the empty cardboard box, hoping Rugbee would find it while she was gone.

When she got to the beach, she quickly spotted the little redheaded girl in the water. As she watched her grandmother diving under the waves, she wondered if the formula had finished working and if Emma Brown would remain this age. She thought of her parents, and her nose began to wrinkle. A thirty-year-old grandmother, well, maybe they could have gotten used to it. A fifteen-year-old would have been hard, but a ten-year-old, especially this ten-year-old, would be impossible for them to accept!

"Come on, Nell," Emmy called from the water, "let's play shells."

The words rang in Nelly's ears above the roar of the surf. She suddenly remembered the time her grandmother first told her about playing shells. That was the night Nelly had decided to invent the formula. It had seemed like such a good idea then. Tears welled up in her eyes as she remembered her grandmother's soothing voice, her creaking rocking chair, and the cozy closeness between them on those first two nights in the cottage.

Emmy came up to Nelly and took her hand. Together they lay down and let the waves carry them back and forth.

"We're free, we're free." Emmy Brown laughed as her wet hair glistened in the sunlight.

Nelly closed her eyes and tried to remember again what her grandmother's voice used to sound like. But this time she couldn't. "I miss you. I miss you, Grandma," she whispered, as the redheaded girl squeezed her hand. A giant wave picked them up and sent them sailing all the way up onto the beach.

Chapter 12

Nelly had a hard time getting Emmy to come out of the water.

"Come on, let's get out now. I want to check on Rugbee," Nelly called to her as she came up from under a wave.

"No, I want to stay in and swim," Emmy answered, lying back in the water.

"We can come again later," Nelly told her, but Emmy just ignored her and continued to dive in and out of the waves. "We can walk to the bakery for doughnuts," Nelly coaxed.

"What kind of doughnuts?" Emmy wanted to know.

"What kind do you like?" Nelly asked.

"Jelly." Emmy grinned. "I love jelly dough-nuts."

"That's what we'll get, then, but we'd better

leave now before the bakery is all out of them. It's getting late," Nelly said, steering Emmy toward the shore.

As they walked on the beach, they came across a man and a woman sound asleep on a blanket. There was an umbrella attached to a basket next to them, with the words DO NOT DISTURB scribbled on it.

"I wonder what's under there?" Emmy whispered. Before Nelly could stop her, she lifted the umbrella to have a look. A baby had just fallen asleep inside the basket. Suddenly, he let out a howl that made Emmy jump, sending the umbrella flying over to the sleeping man.

"Hey, what are you girls doing?" the angry man demanded.

"Sorry," Emmy called, as she ran back into the water, leaving Nelly behind.

"Grandma, get back here!" Nelly called, making the man not only angry but confused.

"Grandma . . . er, Emmy get over here!" Nelly ran to the edge of the water and stood with her hands on her hips. Emmy finally came out, and they walked back to the cottage, Nelly lecturing all the way.

"I can't take my eyes off you for a minute," she was saying.

"I just wanted to see what was under the umbrella. Don't you ever get curious?" Emmy had stopped to pick up an empty potato chip bag on the beach. She looked to see if there were any potato chips left inside.

"Of course I get curious. I'm going to be a scientist when I grow up, but you have to investigate like a scientist, not like a kid," Nelly explained.

"But I am a kid." Emmy Brown frowned.

"Yeah, you sure are." Nelly sighed, taking the potato chip bag away from Emmy and throwing it in a trash can. "Come on, I'll get some money and then we'll walk over to the bakery for doughnuts. Oh, but first I have to find Rugbee."

While Emmy played with Nelly's skateboard on the porch, Nelly searched for Rugbee. She looked all over the cottage, under beds and tables and behind chairs and bookcases, but she couldn't find him anywhere.

"Rugbee, Rugbee, here, boy," Nelly called. After searching the entire cottage and finding no sign of the puppy, Nelly slumped down in a chair at the kitchen table. Where could Rugbee be? What could have happened to him?

"Oh, no," Nelly groaned, as she thought about what had been happening to her grandmother. If the effects of the formula were speeding up, then Rugbee would be quite a bit younger than the puppy that he was last night. But how could he get any younger? If he got any younger he wouldn't be born yet! Nelly sank down into a kitchen chair. She couldn't believe it. She couldn't believe what she had done!

"Oh, Rugbee, I'm so sorry. I never meant to do this to you, really I didn't," she whispered, as she stared down at his empty doggy dish on the floor.

It was true, Rugbee was gone, vanished. The formula had worked so well that he had just kept getting younger and younger until he'd finally stopped existing!

"It's like he's dead and I killed him," Nelly said aloud. Tears filled her eyes as she sat remembering the way things used to be. Everything was so different now. She could no longer hear Rugbee's low comforting snores and his old doggy yawns. She missed his big sad sleepy eyes. And the kitchen seemed so empty without the soft humming of her grandmother at the stove and the aroma of something warm and sweet just out of the oven. There was a strange stillness in the cottage that made Nelly feel terribly alone.

"Whoopee!" The shrieks of Emmy Brown's squeaky voice broke the silence. She had gone into the bedroom and was jumping on the bed again.

Listening to the creaking bedsprings, Nelly's face went white. She suddenly realized that if her grandmother kept getting younger, she would end up like Rugbee! Vanished! Gone forever! Nelly sat with her head in her hands, feeling as if she were the only person in the world with this terrible secret. She had to talk to someone. If only she had a friend, an ally. Ben!

Nelly looked at the calendar on the refrigerator, and her face brightened. Her grandmother had circled the twenty-third and had written under it, "Meet Ben at the bus stop, 9:00 A.M." Nelly checked the days of the week. Today was the twenty-second so Ben was coming tomorrow! She was so relieved that she even managed to smile. Ben would know what to do. Together they would come up with something to fix this mess. She'd just have to keep an eye on her grandmother till Ben got here. Nelly sighed. She had a feeling that that wasn't going to be easy.

Chapter 13

Nelly was right. It was no easy task keeping an eye on her grandmother. After a few minutes, Emmy Brown grew bored with jumping on the bed and decided to try out Nelly's skateboard in the living room. Nelly jumped when she heard the lamp go crashing to the floor!

"Can't you stay out of trouble for even a minute?" Nelly scolded, as she helped her grandmother up from the floor.

"It wasn't my fault," Emmy complained. "I was trying to skate around the corner but the footstool was in the way."

"Skateboards are not meant to be used inside," Nelly said, taking the skateboard away from her.

"Just let me use it a little longer. I know I can get good at this thing. I know I can."

"You can practice on the way to the bakery, and if you get good enough, I'll let you skate to the post office later." Nelly went into her grandmother's bedroom and got her wallet out of her purse. She counted out thirty-three dollars. That would certainly be enough for the doughnuts.

Emmy practiced skateboarding the three blocks to the bakery, with Nelly close behind her. Suddenly she jumped off the skateboard in front of a little shop. She put her face to the window as Nelly came up next to her.

"Boy, I'd love to have one of those," she sighed, pointing to a rack of different-colored baseball caps.

Nelly smiled to herself. She couldn't help remembering all the times she had shopped with her grandmother and had said those exact same words. Her grandmother had usually given in and bought her what she wanted.

"OK, Em, I guess I owe you one," Nelly said, handing her some money. In a few minutes, a grinning Emmy Brown came walking out of the store with her curly red hair falling out of the bright green baseball cap. Together they walked the rest of the way to the bakery, talking about skateboards, baseball, and jelly doughnuts.

"I could eat a dozen jelly doughnuts!"
Emmy declared, as they entered the bakery
and got a whiff from the doughnut counter.

"A whole dozen? You couldn't eat a whole
dozen, you'd get sick," Nelly told her.

"No, I wouldn't get sick because when I
love something I really love it and eating a
dozen jelly doughnuts would be heaven."
Emmy closed her eyes and seemed to go into
a swoon.

Nelly couldn't help smiling. Even though
this Emmy Brown was a pain and a whole lot
of trouble, she was fun to be around.

"Listen, how much do you like jelly doughnuts? Do you love them?" Emmy asked.

"Well, yeah, I guess I do," Nelly admitted.

"Then why have just a nibble when you can
have a whole dozen?" Emmy leaned against
the counter and rolled her eyes.

Nelly had never eaten a dozen jelly doughnuts before, but maybe it was an opportunity
she shouldn't pass up.

"Two dozen jelly doughnuts, please," she
told the man behind the counter.

"You're not planning on eating these all
yourself, are you?" the friendly man joked.

"Oh, no, my grandmother is going to help
me," Nelly replied with a grin. They walked

the rest of the way home, taking turns on the skateboard and stuffing their mouths with jelly doughnuts. Nelly smiled as they walked past the bus station.

It's going to be OK, she thought to herself. Ben will be here tomorrow and everything will be OK.

By the time they reached the cottage, they were both moaning. They had managed to eat eleven doughnuts each, and the thought of having to eat one more made them groan. They went inside and stretched out on Nelly's bed, holding their stomachs.

When Nelly finally got up to work in her lab, Emmy insisted on accompanying her.

"I can be your assistant," Emmy told her.

Nelly shook her head. "This is serious stuff. These aren't toys I'm playing with," she said sternly. "You can sit quietly and watch, but don't touch anything."

Emmy smiled, her blue eyes twinkling as she looked at all the glassware.

Nelly assumed her serious scientist look and took down a beaker from the shelf. She measured in some baking soda and then added some white vinegar from a special tall bottle that had a glass stopper. She added a few drops of green food coloring and a squirt of dish soap.

She sneaked a look at Emmy, who was thoroughly enthralled. Nelly felt very important, even though she knew that this certainly wouldn't undo the formula.

"Wow, how did you do that?" Emmy asked, as the green bubbling liquid in the beaker foamed up to the top and over onto the table.

"It's not as easy as it looks," Nelly assured her. "I've been working at being a scientist for a long time. These experiments that I'm doing are not for beginners."

Just then the phone started ringing in the cottage. Emmy jumped up. "You stay right here. I'll answer it," Nelly told her. "It's probably Mom and Dad. Stay here and don't touch anything," she called over her shoulder as she ran out of the lab.

Nelly was right. It was her mother on the phone. She asked how Nelly was doing and then she asked about Grandma.

"Grandma? Oh, she's fine. We walked to the bakery this morning for jelly doughnuts, then we came home and took a nap. Now she's out in my lab. I'm showing her some of my experiments. Do you think you could talk to her the next time you call? We're kind of in the middle of an experiment." Nelly held her breath, waiting for her mother's answer. She had no idea what she would do if her mother insisted on talking to Grandma.

"It sounds like you two are busy, so I won't bother you. Just tell Grandma that we'll talk to her the next time we call. I'm glad to hear that everything is all right. How is Rugbee doing? I bet he loves being at the beach," her mother said.

"Rugbee? Oh, Rugbee! You know how sleepy he is. You hardly know he's around." Nelly wondered if her mother was going to ask her to put Rugbee on the phone. She was relieved when she didn't.

"I've got an incredible sunburn, but it was worth it. We spent most of yesterday out on a boat taking samples. The project is really going well. Your father and I both miss you, Nell, but we're glad that you're having this time with Grandma. Be good and we'll call again in a day or two."

Nelly hung up the phone and sighed. She knew that if the formula kept working Grandma would be talking baby talk the next time her parents called.

"I've got to do something," Nelly groaned. "I've got to get back to the lab and come up with something that will reverse the effects of the formula, otherwise Grandma will end up like Rugbee!" She opened the screen door to go outside. That's when she first smelled the smoke!

Chapter 14

"**O**h, no!" Nelly cried, as she looked up to see smoke pouring out of the little window in her lab.

"Good grief, Grandma, what have you done now?" she cried, racing to the shed. Nelly peered in to see most of her bottles of chemicals on the table. A small fire had started next to her Bunsen burner and there was no sign of Emmy. Nelly ran to the cottage and got the fire extinguisher from the kitchen. Her father had taught her how to use it when he had given her her first Bunsen burner.

Nelly tried to stay calm and remember everything her father had told her. With a shaky hand, she held the extinguisher and sprayed what seemed to be a burning roll of paper towels. There was smoke everywhere, but still no sign of Emmy Brown. After she was sure she'd put the fire out, Nelly slumped against the doorway. She closed her eyes and took a deep breath of fresh air. Suddenly Emmy came tearing around the corner with a bucket of water. Without looking, she threw the water into the lab, soaking Nelly's face!

"Oh, gosh, I'm sorry!" Emmy cried. "I was just trying to put out the fire."

"The fire is out, no thanks to you," Nelly fumed, trying to shake herself dry. "For someone who was told not to touch anything, you managed to rearrange all my chemicals and start a fire! From now on, we're staying out of the lab until Ben comes."

Back at the cottage, Nelly fixed them some peanut butter and jelly sandwiches. There was no television set so they looked through the games that Nelly had brought up from the cellar. They set up the old checkerboard. While Nelly was in the bathroom, Emmy replaced all the checkers with pieces of pepperoni. Nelly had to admit that it made for a better game. Every time you jumped a piece of pepperoni you got to eat it! After they had played for a long time and gone through a whole pound of pepperoni, they decided that they were too stuffed to play anymore.

They went back outside, and Emmy begged Nelly to let her use her skateboard.

"You promised I could take it to the post office," she whined.

"Well, OK, but don't talk to anyone and don't go anywhere else. If you get in trouble one more time, I won't let you get on my skateboard anymore. Do you understand?" Nelly tried to sound as stern as her mother when she lectured Nelly.

She gave Emmy the key and the number of their postbox. "It's just a block up from the bakery," she told her. "I'll be waiting right here on the porch. You will stay out of trouble this time, won't you?" Nelly almost pleaded.

"I'll be on my best behavior." Emmy grinned.

As Emmy Brown took off down the lane with the skateboard under her arm, Nelly stood on the porch, watching. She remembered her grandmother as she used to be, her old grandmother, then she thought of her at age thirty, at age fifteen, and now at age ten.

Suddenly Nelly had an idea. She ran into the cottage, grabbed the camera off her dresser, and an apple off the kitchen table. She walked down to the end of the lane and waited for Emmy to return.

After quite a while, Nelly could see the slight figure of her grandmother on top of her skateboard. As Emmy came into view, Nelly tried adjusting the focus. Nelly's nose wrinkled. Did her grandmother seem shorter, as she skated toward her, or was it just the camera that made her seem that way? When she called to Emmy to say cheese, she had no doubt that her grandmother had shrunk!

Oh, no! It's not the camera! Nelly mumbled to herself. It's the formula! Not only was Emmy Brown much shorter, with her bathing suit three sizes too big, but she was also missing her two front teeth!

Oh, Grandma, Nelly was thinking, you don't even look like a ten-year-old anymore! You look like you're six!

That night, Nelly lay in bed for a long time listening to the waves outside her bedroom window. She remembered her grandmother telling her that there was no music as beautiful as the lullaby of the ocean. Nelly missed hearing things like that, things only her grandmother would say. Again, she tried to remember her grandmother's seventy-year-old voice, old and low and comforting. It was the voice of someone who had lived a long time and was glad she had. It was the kind of voice that you

wanted to hear when you weren't sure of things, or when you were feeling all alone.

"I can't sleep," came the small voice of a child in the dark. It was Emmy. She had come up beside Nelly's bed and was tugging at her pillow. Nelly moved over, making room for her in the bed.

"I'm afraid," the little redheaded girl whispered in the darkness.

"I know," Nelly whispered back. "Me, too." Together, they lay in the big double bed listening to the ocean's lullaby coming in through the open window until they both drifted off to sleep.

Chapter 15

When Nelly opened her eyes, it was morning and the cottage was quiet. Completely quiet. She yawned and thought about rolling over and going back to sleep. Instead, she sat up straight in bed. Quiet? Why was it so quiet? Roll over? How could she roll over if Emmy was in bed with her? But as she looked down beside her, Nelly was filled with horror. The bed was empty. Emmy was gone!

The stillness of the cottage gripped her. She couldn't believe it. Her grandmother was gone! Vanished like Rugbee!

"Grandma, where are you? Where have you gone? What have I done?" Nelly fought back tears as she walked through the empty rooms. She stood in the hallway, listening to the soft drone of the refrigerator in the kitchen. She wiped away a tear and stepped on a Cheerio. It made a crunching noise under her foot. She didn't think much about it until she stepped on a second and then a third Cheerio. Looking down, she noticed a trail of Cheerios going from the kitchen into the living room. She followed the trail to the coffee table, where it came to a stop. Suddenly, she heard a loud crunching noise.

Nelly bent down and found a chubby red-headed child of about four years old happily eating from a box of cereal. Nelly's face lit up at the sight of her.

"Grandma! Is it you? Is it really you?"

The little Emmy Brown laughed and threw a Cheerio, hitting Nelly on the nose.

"Now, I'm sure it's you!" Nelly laughed with relief. "Come on, we'll get some breakfast." Nelly took Emmy's chubby little hand in hers, and they walked into the kitchen. "You spilled most of the cereal on the floor, so we'll have to have something else for breakfast," Nelly told her, standing on a chair and looking through the kitchen cabinets. Then Nelly got down and opened the refrigerator.

"How about some eggs?" she asked.

But Emmy stuck out her tongue and held her nose.

"I guess that's a no." Nelly laughed. "Well, I really don't know how to cook eggs, anyway, so let's see what else we have. I know, how about my specialty, peanut butter and jelly sandwiches?"

Emmy grinned and shook her head up and down. "I love jelly sandwiches," she said, her bright red curls bouncing about her face.

Nelly smiled. "I kind of figured that. But you have to have them with peanut butter so you get some protein. We learned that when we studied nutrition in school. But I guess you haven't been to school. You're so little you probably haven't done much of anything yet."

Emmy made a face and stuck out her tongue. "I'm not little," she quipped. "I'm a big girl." Then she climbed up on the table and stood as straight as she could. Nelly tried not to laugh at the sight of her bathing suit falling down around Emmy's chubby knees.

"OK, OK, you're a big kid," Nelly relented. "Now, sit down while I finish making these sandwiches."

Nelly was about to sit down herself, when she heard the phone ringing. "Oh, no," she moaned, "it's probably Mom and Dad. What am I going to tell them when they want to talk to you?" But Emmy didn't answer. She was too busy dipping her fingers into the jelly jar. Nelly walked into the living room and stood by the phone. Maybe she could just let it ring. Her parents would think that she and Grandma were up at the beach. But then they'd just call back later. No, she'd have to talk to them.

She picked up the phone and said a very quiet "Hello."

"Where are you?" a familiar voice said on the other end.

"Ben! Ben, where are *you?* Oh, my gosh, I forgot, it's today!" Nelly cried.

"Yeah, it usually is today." Her cousin laughed. "I thought you and Grandma were supposed to meet me here."

"You're here, already? Oh, Ben, I'm sorry. I got up late, and I thought Emmy was gone. She wasn't in my bed, so I thought she ended up like Rugbee . . ."

"Rugbee? Huh? What are you talking about?" Ben interrupted.

"Oh, Ben, I have so much to tell you." Nelly suddenly felt like crying.

"Well, wait till I get there. Tell Grandma that I'm here, and you two can come and pick me up."

"About Grandma, Ben. There's something I have to tell you. You see . . . well, I guess I can wait until I see you. The cottage is just a few blocks from where you are. We'll be right there," Nelly told him.

When she got to the kitchen, she saw that Emmy's face and hands were completely covered with jelly. She even had jelly on her toes!

"For a little kid, you sure can make some big messes," Nelly sighed.

"I'm a big kid," Emmy mumbled, her fingers in her mouth.

"Yeah, yeah, you're a big kid," Nelly said, trying to wipe off some of the jelly. "But you're not big enough to fit into my bathing suit anymore. I don't have any smaller ones, so I guess we'll just have to fix this one." She went to her grandmother's sewing basket and took out a safety pin. Nelly bunched up as much of the bathing suit as she could from the back and pinned it.

"That looks better," she said, surveying Emmy from the front and trying not to notice the bunched-up mess in the back. "Now come on, I'll take you for a ride in the wagon." Nelly got out the wagon that had been behind the shed. Emmy jumped right in. When they finally got to the bus station, Nelly's face brightened at the sight of her cousin.

"Hi, Ben. Boy, am I glad to see you!" Nelly

said, reaching out to help him with his skateboard.

"Yeah, I'm glad to be off that bus. It took
forever to get here. Who's that?" he asked,
looking over at the wagon.

"Her name is Emmy," Nelly began.

"I'm a big kid," Emmy told him, standing
up in the wagon. But as she did, the wheels
turned and she began to fall. Ben quickly
reached out to grab her and ended up with
jelly all over his shirt.

"Oh, great," he groaned. "Mom wanted me
to wear this shirt because Grandma gave it to
me. Now look at it!"

"Uh, I don't think Grandma will mind,"
Nelly said quietly.

"Hey, where is Grandma, anyway?" Ben
asked, looking around.

"Right there," Nelly said, pointing to the
wagon.

"Right where?" Ben wanted to know.

"There in the wagon." Nelly winced as she
pointed to Emmy, who was trying to get her
foot in her mouth so she could suck the jelly off
her toes.

"Nelly, what are you talking about?" Ben
picked up his suitcase and looked around the
bus station.

Nelly started pulling the wagon toward the cottage. "You see, I made this special formula and poured it on Grandma's hair . . ."

"Oh, I get it. You invented a formula that turned Grandma invisible, and she's sitting in the wagon behind the little kid with jelly on her toes."

"I'm a big kid," Emmy interrupted, lifting up her head.

"Well, not exactly," Nelly tried to explain. "Grandma *is* that little kid in the wagon with jelly on her toes."

"Yeah, and I'm Santa Claus."

Nelly sighed. She wondered if Madame Curie ever had to convince people that the impossible could be possible. She supposed that it happened all the time when you were a scientist.

Patience, Nelly thought. Madame Curie must have had lots and lots of patience. "Let me start at the beginning, Ben. You see, I found this old chemistry set in the cellar . . ."

Chapter 16

It took Nelly the entire walk home to explain everything to Ben, but he was not convinced.

"Grandma, where are you?" he called, following Nelly and Emmy into the cottage.

"Ben, I told you, she's right here," Nelly said, getting a drink of water for Emmy from the sink.

"Come on, Nell, I know she's up on the beach. I'm going to change into my bathing suit, and then we'll find her." Ben went into the bathroom to change.

"Whatever you say, Ben, but I'm telling you, she's not there."

When Ben came out of the bathroom, the three of them went up to the beach and Ben looked on every blanket and in every beach chair.

"She must be in the water," he said, walking toward the surf.

It was high tide and the ocean was rough with choppy waves. There were only a few people swimming.

"There she is." Ben pointed to a silver-haired woman who was diving under a wave. Nelly let go of Emmy's hand and ran up next to Ben. The woman did look a lot like Emma Brown from the back, but as she came up out of the waves, Ben could see that she was definitely not their grandmother.

"I told you," Nelly said.

"Maybe you've been without TV for too long, Nell. You're starting to make up these fantastic stories." Ben shook his head in disgust.

"Stories?" Nelly was insulted. "I'm a scientist, Ben. I deal with facts. You know I don't make up stories. If it's just a story, then where is Grandma?"

"That's easy," Ben told her. "She's probably shopping. We'll go back to the cottage, and she'll be there."

"Oh, Ben, I wish you'd believe me. She's not there because she's right . . ." Nelly looked down beside her and suddenly realized that Emmy had disappeared.

"Now, where has she gone?" Nelly looked across the beach, but there was no sign of the chubby little redheaded girl. "Oh, my gosh! I hope she didn't try and go in the water. She can't be old enough to swim yet," Nelly cried, running back to the water's edge.

"Who's kid is she, anyway?" Ben could see that Nelly was upset.

"She's Emmy. Emmy like in Emma, like in Emma Brown. Get it? She's your grandmother and she's not old enough to swim and why did I ever let go of her hand?"

Ben didn't say anything, but he was beginning to get the strange feeling that Nelly might be telling the truth. This is just too weird, he thought. Together, the two of them walked up and down the beach calling Emmy's name. They began asking people if they'd seen her, but no one had. They were about to give up when Nelly spotted something on a blanket under an umbrella. It was a bunched-up blue bathing suit with a pin in it. The little redheaded girl wearing it was fast asleep.

Nelly let out a sigh of relief. "Come on, you can take a nap at home," she told Emmy, helping her to her feet.

Back at the cottage, Ben began calling for their grandmother again. But the cottage was empty and as Nelly pointed out, Emma Brown's car was still in the driveway.

Ben had to admit that this was strange. "And she did tell me that she would meet me at the bus stop," he said out loud.

Nelly had just walked into the living room, after putting Emmy down for a nap on her bed. "You see, it's true. Everything I've been telling you is true. Come on out to my lab. I want to show you something."

They went to the shed, and Nelly got out the old chemistry set. "Wow, this is great," Ben said, looking it over. He was as impressed as Nelly had been when she first saw it. He grew quiet as he read through the book. His mouth dropped open when he read the list of formulas at the back.

"You mean you weren't joking? You actually thought that you could make a formula that would turn Grandma . . ." But he was suddenly interrupted by a loud crash coming from the cottage.

"She's up," Nelly groaned, "and when she's awake she's trouble." Nelly and Ben headed for the cottage. When they opened the screen door and looked inside the kitchen, they gasped at the sight that met their eyes. All of the bottom kitchen cabinets were open and the contents had been emptied out onto the floor. There were pots and pans and cans of food everywhere. But it wasn't the mess that made them gasp. It was the sight of Emmy Brown, sitting in the middle of it all, sucking her thumb. She had gotten shorter, a lot shorter, and there was so much baby fat on her that her eyes looked like two little blue dots. She couldn't be more than two years old.

"But . . . but that can't be the same kid," Ben stammered.

"Sure it is. Look, she crawled right out of her bathing suit. Oh, she's almost a baby!" Nelly groaned.

"But what's happened to her? How did she get like that?" Ben couldn't believe his eyes.

"It's like I told you, it's the formula. And if it keeps on working, she's going to end up just like Rugbee." Nelly sighed.

The two of them stood staring, unable to move. They watched as the little redheaded toddler picked up a jar of spaghetti sauce and hurled it across the kitchen. It hit the stove and broke, sending thick red sauce everywhere.

"Do you believe her? She's almost a baby, and she still manages to make a giant mess!" Nelly moaned as she reached down to pick Emmy up.

"This is incredible! This is just too incredible!" Ben stood mumbling, as Nelly handed the toddler to him. He sat down at the kitchen table with the chubby little Emmy in his lap. She was bending over his arm, licking some leftover jelly off the tablecloth.

"What do you think, Ben? Do you think we can come up with something that can reverse the formula before it's too late?" Nelly looked up from the floor where she was picking up broken glass.

"We're going to have to, Nell. But first we need some diapers, because I don't think Grandma is potty-trained." He sighed, looking down at the yellow stream that was suddenly trickling down his leg!

Chapter 17

Nelly rode her skateboard into town to buy Pampers, while Ben cleaned up the kitchen. Emmy wandered around, stepping in spaghetti sauce and wiping her sticky fingers on everything she touched. Ben finally got the kitchen cleaned. Then he picked up Emmy and carried her into the bathroom. He turned on the water in the tub.

"Come on," he said, "it's time for a swim." But she would have none of it and kicked him in the shins.

"Ouch! Grandma, I'm surprised at you. After all the times you've told me to never kick anyone!" Ben looked on the bathroom shelves. "I know," he said, "how about some bubbles?" He found a box of bubble bath and poured a little into the tub. He put the box on the floor and swirled the water around with his hands. Emmy clapped her hands and grinned.

"Bubbas, bubbas," she cried happily in her baby voice.

Just then Nelly came back with the box of Pampers. "Boy, I'm glad you're here to help me," she said, opening up the Pampers bag.

"Yeah, it's funny. The last thing my mom said to me before I got on the bus was, 'I know you'll be a big help to your grandmother, and don't get in any trouble.' "

"Talk about trouble." Nelly sighed.

"Bubbas, bubbas," Emmy Brown laughed, as Ben put her in the tub. She threw a handful of bubbles in the air, and they landed on her head. Nelly and Ben laughed, too.

"You have to admit, she's awfully cute for a grandmother," Ben said. He wiped Emmy's face with a washcloth, and she bit his finger. "Hey, I take that back. Make that awfully dangerous for a grandmother."

They were about to take Emmy out of the tub when the phone rang.

"Oh, no! It's them!" Nelly cried.

"Who?" Ben asked.

"My parents. They called yesterday, and I told them Grandma was busy with me in the lab. They'll want to talk to her for sure this time. What should I do?"

"Well, the only thing I've heard Grandma say lately is 'bubbas,' and I don't think your parents are going to want to make that kind of conversation. Let me talk to them," Ben said, standing up.

"What are you going to say?" Nelly looked worried.

"I'll just tell them the truth," Ben said, walking into the living room.

"The truth! No, Ben, you can't! They won't believe it, and even if they do, they'll kill me!" Nelly cried. But it was too late, Ben had already picked up the phone.

"Hello? Oh, hi, Uncle Mark, it's me, Ben. Yes I got here this morning. Nelly and Grandma met me at the bus stop . . . How are we doing? Uh, it's awesome, Uncle Mark, really awesome." Ben rolled his eyes. "Grandma? Well, to tell you the truth, Uncle Mark . . ." He stopped and looked over at Nelly, who was shaking her head violently. Ben smiled. "To tell you the truth, she's taking a bath."

Nelly sank down on the rocking chair and closed her eyes. After Ben had talked for a while, he handed her the phone. She assured her father that they "were having an incredible time." She also told him that she would tell Grandma that he'd be calling back tomorrow night.

"That was close," Nelly said, hanging up the phone. "They're calling back tomorrow and this time they'll insist on talking to Grandma." She frowned.

"Nell, if that formula keeps working, there won't be a grandma by tomorrow," Ben said gravely.

"You're right. We've got to work on a new formula." Nelly turned around and walked toward the kitchen. "Let's go out to my lab and see what we can come up with."

"Uh, aren't you forgetting someone?" Ben said, pointing to the bathroom.

"Oh, my gosh, Grandma!" Nelly turned and hurried into the bathroom, but there was no sign of the chubby two-year-old anywhere. Instead, there were bubbles, lots and lots of bubbles pouring out of the bathtub.

"She must have turned the water on full blast and dumped in the whole box of bubbles!" Nelly cried. Ben spotted little soapy footprints leading out of the bathroom and into the kitchen.

"You take care of this mess, and I'll go find her," Ben said.

While Nelly turned off the faucets and cleaned up the bathroom, Ben followed the footprints. Nelly heard the screen door slam and went into the kitchen. "Ben, did you find her?" she called into the backyard.

"We're out here, Nell, in your lab. Bring a diaper!" Ben answered. He had found Emmy sitting precariously on the little table in the lab. She had climbed up a chair and was happily cooing, as she held up some of the bottles from the old chemistry set.

"Oh, no you don't," Ben said, taking the bottles away from her. "You've gotten into enough trouble," he told her. He picked her up and placed her on the old raft that he'd taken down from the wall. Emmy closed her eyes and seemed to fall asleep.

Nelly came in with a Pamper and tried putting it on the sleeping child. "Do you believe the trouble she gets into?" she whispered, struggling with the Pamper.

"After all this, I think I'd believe just about anything," Ben said, sitting down on the edge of the raft. He looked over at Nelly who began setting out a beaker on her lab table.

"What are you doing?" he asked her.

"I'm just making up a solution of super dish soap. I make it for Grandma all the time, not that she'd be too interested in it now, except for the bubbles." Nelly sighed.

"Nelly, that's just great. You're making dish soap for someone who's not even old enough to wash a dish! Isn't that a waste of time, when you should be trying to come up with a new formula to get things back to normal?"

"No, it's not a waste of time, Ben. It's the way I work. Sometimes, by just mixing chemicals I get a feel for formulas. I was hoping it would work this time," Nelly explained.

"Is it working?" Ben asked.

"No, but this looks like the best dish soap that I've ever made."

"Great, Nell, great!" Ben sounded exasperated.

"Why don't you look through the old instruction book once more," Nelly suggested. "There's got to be something in there to help us."

As Nelly continued to mix chemicals, Ben read and reread the old book. He finally closed it, shaking his head.

"There's just no mention of reversing the formula anywhere in here," he moaned.

"Well, how about the company that makes

McFinney's Powerful Potions? Maybe we could get them to help us," Nelly said.

"We don't have time to write but maybe we could call them," Ben suggested, turning the book over to look for an address. When he didn't find one he got up and looked on the box. "Here's something on the back, but the letters are so small, they're hard to read."

He carried the box to the window and while Nelly looked over his shoulder, he read the tiny print.

MCFINNEY'S POWERFUL POTIONS IS A PRODUCT OF MCFINNEY'S MAGNIFICENT MYSTERIES CO. OF MIS-TLETOE, KANSAS, U.S.A.

"That's it," Nelly cried.

"All we have to do is call information and get the number of McFinney's Magnificent Mysteries Company and tell them what happened," Ben said.

"I bet they have some first-rate scientists working for them," Nelly shouted excitedly. "They've got to help us. They've just got to."

Chapter 18

Nelly and Ben were both so excited that they jumped up and down together and then headed for the door. But Nelly stopped short. She wasn't taking any more chances. She wasn't about to leave her troublesome charge alone again. So Ben waited in the lab with Emmy, while Nelly went into the cottage to call.

She had copied down the name and address of the company, but when she dialed the number for information, she was told that she'd have to dial another number for Kansas information. When she finally got through, she asked the operator for the number of Mc-Finney's Magnificent Mysteries Co. in Mistletoe. The operator got back on and told her that she had nothing under that listing.

"Nothing?" Nelly asked. "Are you sure?"

"Sorry, nothing under that listing," the operator said again. "I do have something for McFinney's Magnificent Mattress Company in Mistletoe, though. Would you like to try that?" the operator asked.

"OK," Nelly said weakly, "I guess so." She didn't really think a mattress company could help her but she didn't know where else to turn. She dialed the number, and the voice of an old woman answered.

"McFinney's Magnificent Mattress Company. Miss McFinney speaking, how may I help you?"

"Uh, well, I was looking for another McFinney, actually. And I thought you might know the number. McFinney's Magnificent Mysteries Company," Nelly told her.

"Oh, my stars! And who might you be, dear?" the old woman exclaimed.

"My name is Nelly, Nelly Brown and I . . ."

"Now just hold on while I get out the ledger," the old woman interrupted. "Let me see, Bellini, Blitzen, Block . . . must be farther down, Brazer, Brentano, Brown, here we are, Brown, Nelly Brown. Yes, dear, your name is in the ledger, and I hope you've enjoyed our product," the old woman said sweetly.

"Well . . ." Nelly was too surprised to answer. Why did this old woman have her name in a ledger? Did she know about the chemistry set?

"You see, Miss McFinney, I made up this formula from McFinney's Powerful Potions and it worked . . ." Nelly began.

"Of course it did, dear," Miss McFinney interrupted. "All of our sets were guaranteed to work or your money back," she said proudly.

"But I thought you were a mattress company?" Nelly was confused.

"Well," the old woman sighed, "in business you have to move with the times. The market for mysteries fell off several years ago and so we went into the mattress business. People love to sleep, you know. Business is booming."

"Oh, but do the scientists that made up the chemistry sets still work for you?" Nelly asked.

Miss McFinney laughed. "Scientists? No, we don't have any scientists working for us. We have mattress makers. That makes sense, don't you think, considering the business we're in?"

"Yes, I guess it does, but do you have the phone number of someone I could call? Someone who worked on making up the formulas?"

The line grew quiet and then the old woman's voice came back on. "I'm afraid not, dear. You see McFinney's Magnificent Mysteries was a family business. It's been in our family for ages. The secret formulas were passed down from generation to generation. My great-great-great-great-grandmother learned the secrets from her father and he passed them down until they finally came to my father who passed them down to my sister Geraldine. Geraldine was an alchemist extraordinaire and she could play the accordion like an angel." The old woman sighed heavily. "Now Geraldine is the one you'd want to talk to, but I'm afraid she died some time ago."

"I'm sorry," Nelly said. "But what about you? Do you know anything about the formulas?"

"Heavens no!" Miss McFinney laughed. "I was in charge of sales, you see."

"Oh, then I guess no one can help me." Nelly knew she was about to cry. "Ben and I thought that you might be able to tell us how to undo the formula . . ." Her voice trailed off.

"What's that? Undo the formula? Is that all

you want? Well, why didn't you say so in the first place?"

"You mean you know how to undo the formulas?" Nelly held the phone closer.

"Of course," Miss McFinney told her. "But who is this Ben fellow?" she asked.

"Ben's my cousin."

"Is he over the age of six?" Miss McFinney wanted to know.

"Yes, he's eleven years old. Why?" Nelly asked.

"It's very simple," the old woman began. "The chemistry sets were designed for children over the age of six. Each set is guaranteed to allow one experiment per person. Now, you've already done your experiment so you can't perform another one. But your cousin Ben can. All he has to do is create an experiment with a formula that undoes the one you made."

"Oh, thank you, thank you!" Nelly cried into the phone.

"Certainly, dear, glad to be of assistance. And if you're ever in Mistletoe, do look us up. We have a nice line of new mattresses that do wonders for your back. As an added feature, they assist the sleeper in having all his dreams

come true. Comes with a money back guarantee, of course."

"That sounds very nice, thank you, thank you very much." Nelly hung up the phone and raced back to the lab.

"Ben, Ben," she called, as she opened the shed door, "all we need is the key and we can undo . . ." But Nelly stopped short. Ben was sitting at the table with a baby in his arms. A very tiny baby with just a bit of red fuzz on the top of her head.

"She's going, Nell!" Ben said, fighting back tears. "She's almost gone."

Chapter 19

Nelly had never seen such a tiny baby.

"I didn't know they came that small," she stammered, walking up to the table. "Oh, Ben, we've got to hurry. I don't think Grandma can get any younger than this."

"I know, Nell. Did you get a hold of McFinney's Magnificent what's it called?" Ben asked, putting his grandmother over his shoulder to burp her.

"McFinney's Magnificent Mysteries, well, sort of. I talked to Miss McFinney, and she said that all we have to do is have you make a formula up that will undo the one I made," Nelly told him, reaching for the velvet book. "Here, just write your name after mine," she said, taking the baby from him and handing him the book and a pen from the table.

"OK, but what should I write for the formula?" Ben asked.

"Uh . . . Let's see. . . . How about this? I wish to make a formula that will undo everything that formula 212 did."

"That sounds good," Ben said, writing it into the book. "But what if I just added a little something, like besides undoing the formula, it would also give me extraordinary skateboarding skills?"

Nelly groaned and shifted the baby in her arms. "This is no time to be thinking of yourself, Ben. We've got to hurry. Grandma seems to be getting smaller and smaller. I think the formula's effects have really speeded up!"

Ben looked up and saw that Nelly was right. The baby was definitely shrinking. Ben quickly finished writing out the formula and then turned to page three. He followed the new instructions, mixing and measuring the compounds.

"I'm going to need some seawater, Nell," Ben said, as he took out the large glass beaker.

"I'll get some," Nelly told him, putting the baby down on the raft and running out of the shed with a bucket. When she got back, Ben had just added the last compound to the beaker. He took the bucket from her and mea-

sured out the proper amount of seawater. He stirred it into the beaker and stepped back.

"You had to wait for the other formula to sit overnight," Ben said, watching the bubbling pink liquid.

"I don't think we can wait any longer," Nelly told him, picking up the infant. "I don't think we can wait another minute! I can barely feel her, anymore!"

Ben grabbed the beaker and carried it over to where Nelly was sitting, cradling the now very tiny Emmy Brown in her arms. While Nelly held her, Ben poured the bright pink liquid over Emmy's head. The baby was so small that most of it spilled off her head and onto the floor.

They both looked down at the baby. They held their breaths and waited.

"It's not working, Nell. It's not working!" Ben whispered, his voice choked with tears. Nelly didn't answer. She couldn't since she was too shocked to say a word. Looking down, she could see that he was right. Their grandmother was getting smaller. In fact, she was beginning to fade!

"This is the biggest mistake that I've ever made in my whole life," Nelly Brown moaned.

Chapter 20

Emma Brown was almost gone. Almost, but not quite. Nelly had put the tiny infant back down on the raft. You could see the faded stripes of the raft through her little chest. Both Ben and Nelly were too frightened to move. They waited and waited but there was no further change.

"I think she's hanging on, Nell," Ben finally whispered. "She hasn't gotten any better, but she isn't any worse, either. At least we can still see her, sort of."

"But what if she stays like this!" Nelly cried. "Dad was right. I should never have poured the formula on her."

"What will your folks say when they see her like this?" Ben asked.

Nelly closed her eyes and groaned. "Whatever they'll say, you can bet it will be loud." At that moment, the phone rang in the cottage. "Oh, great! There they are now! I'm dead." Nelly turned toward the door.

"Don't leave me alone with her!" Ben cried. "I mean, what if she should disappear or something?"

"Bring her inside," Nelly told him. "We'll put her in the bedroom, and that way we can keep watch all night, in case there's a change."

While Nelly went to answer the phone, Ben carried the ghostlike infant to the bedroom and gently placed her in the middle of the bed. He went into the kitchen and found Nelly at the refrigerator.

"Was it your parents on the phone?" he asked, sitting down at the table.

"No, it was a wrong number," Nelly said, reaching for a jar of jelly. "But even if we could come up with a way of stalling my parents, we're going to have to tell them pretty soon because we're almost out of money. I spent a lot on those Pampers. I never knew babies were so expensive."

Ben frowned. "I guess that means we can't afford to eat anything fancy tonight. No pizza, huh?"

"Sorry, peanut butter and jelly seems to be

the specialty of the house, only we're out of bread. Here, have a spoon." She smiled, handing him a teaspoon. Together they walked into the bedroom with their jars of peanut butter and jelly. They stood at the edge of the bed, but the sight of the vanishing baby made them feel queasy and unable to eat.

"Maybe we shouldn't stay in here," Ben whispered. "It might make her feel worse."

"That's just what I was thinking," Nelly said, backing toward the door. Neither one of them wanted to admit that they were actually frightened. It was like being in a room with a ghost. A very little ghost!

They went into the living room. Ben stretched out on the couch, while Nelly sat on the braided rug in front of the fireplace.

"I thought this formula would be such a good thing, you know, Ben?" Nelly sat with her head in her hands. "I thought that Grandma would feel so much better. She was getting so old, I was worried. I never thought that I'd be worrying about her getting too young," Nelly sighed.

"It would be great if people could just stay the same," Ben said, yawning. "If we didn't have to change. Maybe you could come up with a formula that would stop a person from changing. Wouldn't it be great to always be a kid?" Ben's eyes lit up.

"Oh, no! If there's one thing I've learned from all this, it's that people are meant to change. It's not something you can fool around with," Nelly said. "But the way people look, now that's something different. Have you ever thought about what you'd look like with hair that glowed in the dark? I've almost got this formula perfected. Just think of what you'd look like on your skateboard, with the sun going down and your head lit up like neon!" Nelly grinned.

Ben groaned and hid his head under a pillow. They stayed up late that night, talking about formulas, and making trips back and forth to the bedroom to check on the ghostlike baby. Their eyes were beginning to close when the clock on the mantle chimed twelve.

"It's your turn to check her," Ben said, yawning from the couch.

Nelly reluctantly pulled herself up from the rug and walked to the bedroom. She closed her eyes as she turned on the light. Each time she'd entered the room, she had been terrified that she would find an empty bed. Poking her head around the door, she was relieved to find the tiny Emmy still curled up between two pillows. But Nelly's relief turned to fear as she lingered in the doorway.

"Please come back, Grandma. Don't end up like Rugbee. I'm sorry. I'm so sorry," Nelly whispered, as she wiped the tears from her eyes. But the fading baby only fluttered her wispy eyelashes, a faint smile still on her face; a face not quite there.

Nelly turned out the light but stood in the doorway, staring. The lace curtains were drawn back and the bed was flooded with moonlight. She stepped up to the edge of the pillows and reached out her hand. The baby turned her head slowly and grasped Nelly's finger, curling her own doll-like fingers around it.

In the stillness of the room, Nelly strained to feel the baby's touch. It was like being grasped by air. She looked down to see the moonlight filtering through the miniature fingers and on to her own hand. In that moment, Nelly knew that her grandmother was saying good-bye. She could sense that Emma Brown wasn't angry or sad. Emma Brown loved her and though Nelly couldn't feel the touch of her grandmother's skin, she could feel the warmth of her heart.

As the wind blew in from the sea, Nelly could smell the damp salt air sifting in through

the screen. She could hear it whistling through the tall grass of the dunes.

A cloud suddenly covered the full moon and in the sudden darkness, Emma Brown un-curled her miniature hand and let go of Nelly's finger. Nelly knew that her grandmother had let go. She couldn't see her. She couldn't touch her. But she knew that her grandmother had let go.

Chapter 21

Nelly and Ben stayed up late that night with all the lights on. They were too afraid to face the dark, and so they sat in the brightly lit living room, waiting for morning.

"I miss her, Ben, I miss her," Nelly cried into her grandmother's cozy cranberry-colored sweater. Nelly had taken it from the rocking chair and covered herself with it as she lay on the rug. "I never meant for this to happen, you know."

"I know, Nell, I know." Ben sighed from the couch. "Try and get some sleep now. It's almost morning." He yawned.

Nelly could hear the wind whistling around the cottage windows. She closed her eyes and snuggled down under the big woolly sweater.

It felt warm and toasty and smelled like cinnamon, her grandmother's favorite spice.

When Nelly awoke the next morning, she sniffed the air. Um, cinnamon, she thought. It was like waking up with her grandmother. Cinnamon muffins and the smell of Emma Brown's fresh pot of coffee meant mornings with Grandma to Nelly. She didn't like the taste of coffee, but she had come to love the scent of it in her grandmother's kitchen.

"Um, smells like she just made it," Nelly mumbled half asleep. Then she took another sniff. Yes, it was definitely cinnamon and coffee, fresh coffee, that she was smelling. Nelly opened her eyes and looked over at the couch. Ben wasn't there. She wondered where he was. He wouldn't be in the kitchen making coffee, would he? No, she knew that Ben hated coffee.

Still wrapped in the big woolly sweater, Nelly got up and made her way to the kitchen. Ben was sitting at the table gulping down orange juice and eating a freshly baked cinnamon muffin. He looked at Nelly with such a large grin that half the muffin fell out of his mouth. Nelly's mouth fell open, too, but it wasn't with a grin. It was the opened-mouth look that you get when you've just seen a ghost or what used to be a ghost!

Standing at the counter, taking some muffins out of the tin, was Emma Brown. The old wrinkly, silvery haired Emma Brown!

"Well, here you are. We thought you were going to sleep the day away," she said in her wonderful old voice.

"Grandma! You're back!" Nelly gasped.

"Back? I didn't know I'd been away." Her grandmother laughed. And so it was. Emma Brown had no memory of the transformation she had been through. She had no recollection of how close she had come to being just a memory herself! Ben's formula had brought her back to her old self as if nothing had been wrong. She didn't even question Ben's arrival but just assumed that she and Nelly had picked him up at the bus station the morning before.

"And tonight, you two are sleeping in beds," their grandmother said firmly. "No more of this living room business. Why, you must have been up talking all night. You look terrible, Nelly," she said, handing her a vitamin.

"Yeah, it was a pretty long night." Ben looked at Nelly and smiled.

"What do you say we rent a boat and do some crabbing out on the bay this afternoon?"

Emma Brown suggested. "That is, if you don't mind spending the afternoon with an old lady."

"Grandma, I'd love to spend the day with an old lady, believe me, I would!" Nelly beamed. It was too good to be true. Her grandmother was back. Her beautiful wrinkly old grandmother, just the way Nelly had remembered her, just the way she had always loved her.

"Now, that's funny, Rugbee hasn't touched the food I put out for him this morning. Have you two seen him anywhere?" Emma Brown looked under the table.

Nelly turned to Ben and bit her lip. Rugbee! How could she tell her grandmother that she had come up with a formula that had sent Rugbee right out of existence! She couldn't. Her grandmother wouldn't believe it, anyway.

"No, I haven't seen him anywhere," said Ben, who always insisted on telling the truth.

Nelly suddenly didn't feel like eating her cinnamon muffin. What had happened to Rugbee? She had thought that since they poured Ben's formula on her grandmother's head, it would undo everything, including Rugbee's disappearance. But Rugbee had not reappeared. Her grandmother looked worried as she went to the door.

"I don't remember letting him out this morning, but maybe I did," Emma Brown said, looking out on the yard. "My memory is just not what it used to be." She shook her head.

"Neither is Rugbee," Ben whispered to Nelly. They finished their breakfast, and Emma Brown began clearing the table.

"Would you two go up to the beach and see if Rugbee's there?" she asked.

Ben shot a look at Nelly. "Sure, Grandma. Come on, Nell," he said, pulling her away from the table.

"What are we going to tell her?" Nelly moaned, as they walked to the dunes.

"The truth," Ben said. "We'll tell her that we went up to the beach and didn't see him anywhere."

Nelly shook her head. She never knew a kid that could tell the truth so much and still not get into trouble. They stayed on the dunes for a long time, Ben stretched out with his eyes closed and Nelly sitting up watching all the people walking along the beach.

"Nobody stays the same," she suddenly said. "And that's not such a bad thing." She was thinking of her grandmother, from the tiny tiny Emmy, all the way to the old Emma

Brown. She suddenly realized that her grandmother had to be all those different Emmas to get to the one she was now, the one Nelly loved best. She had to grow and change. As Nelly buried her feet in the sand, she realized that she would have to change also.

Ben finally got up to leave, and Nelly stood up, too.

"Poor Grandma," Ben said, "she's really going to miss old Rugbee." Nelly could just imagine the look on Emma Brown's face when they told her that they couldn't find him. She began to walk slower and slower. Just as she reached the cottage, she suddenly stopped.

"Did you hear that?" Nelly whispered.

"Hear what?" Ben stood still next to her.

"Listen, it's coming from the kitchen." Nelly walked over to the screen door. Together she and Ben looked in and saw Rugbee, the big old sleepy-looking Rugbee, curled up under the kitchen table, snoring soundly.

"But how did he . . ." Ben stammered.

"Oh, Rugbee!" Nelly cried. "It must take a little longer for dogs to return to their normal state than it does people. Oh, you big beautiful dopey-looking old dog, you're back! Thank goodness you're back!" Rugbee let out a loud yawn and scratched his ear with his paw.

"Oh, here you all are," Emma Brown said, coming into the room. "Well, you've found our wayward dog, I see. This calls for a reward. How about taking a walk to the bakery for some doughnuts to take on our boat trip?"

Nelly looked at Ben. "What kind of doughnuts do you think we should get, Grandma?"

"Um, let me see." Emma Brown closed her eyes a minute. "Jelly doughnuts, I could really go for a few jelly doughnuts," she said.

Nelly looked up with a twinkle in her eye. "Really, just a few?"

Emma Brown's eyebrows went up at this remark. "And just what's that supposed to mean, young lady?" she demanded.

"Tell me something, Grandma, how much do you like jelly doughnuts? Do you love them?" Nelly asked, slipping her hand into her grandmother's. And together they walked down the lane, hand in hand, talking about love and jelly doughnuts.

Ben followed behind them on his skateboard. He was balancing on one foot, doing a high leap in the air, and then coming down perfectly on the other foot.

"Why, Ben," Emma Brown exclaimed, "that's extraordinary!"

"It sure is," Nelly said, giving her cousin a

stern look. Ben quickly jumped off the skateboard with a guilty look. He walked the rest of
the way to the bakery, throwing sticks for Rugbee to chase, but Rugbee just yawned and
stepped slowly over them. Some things never
change.